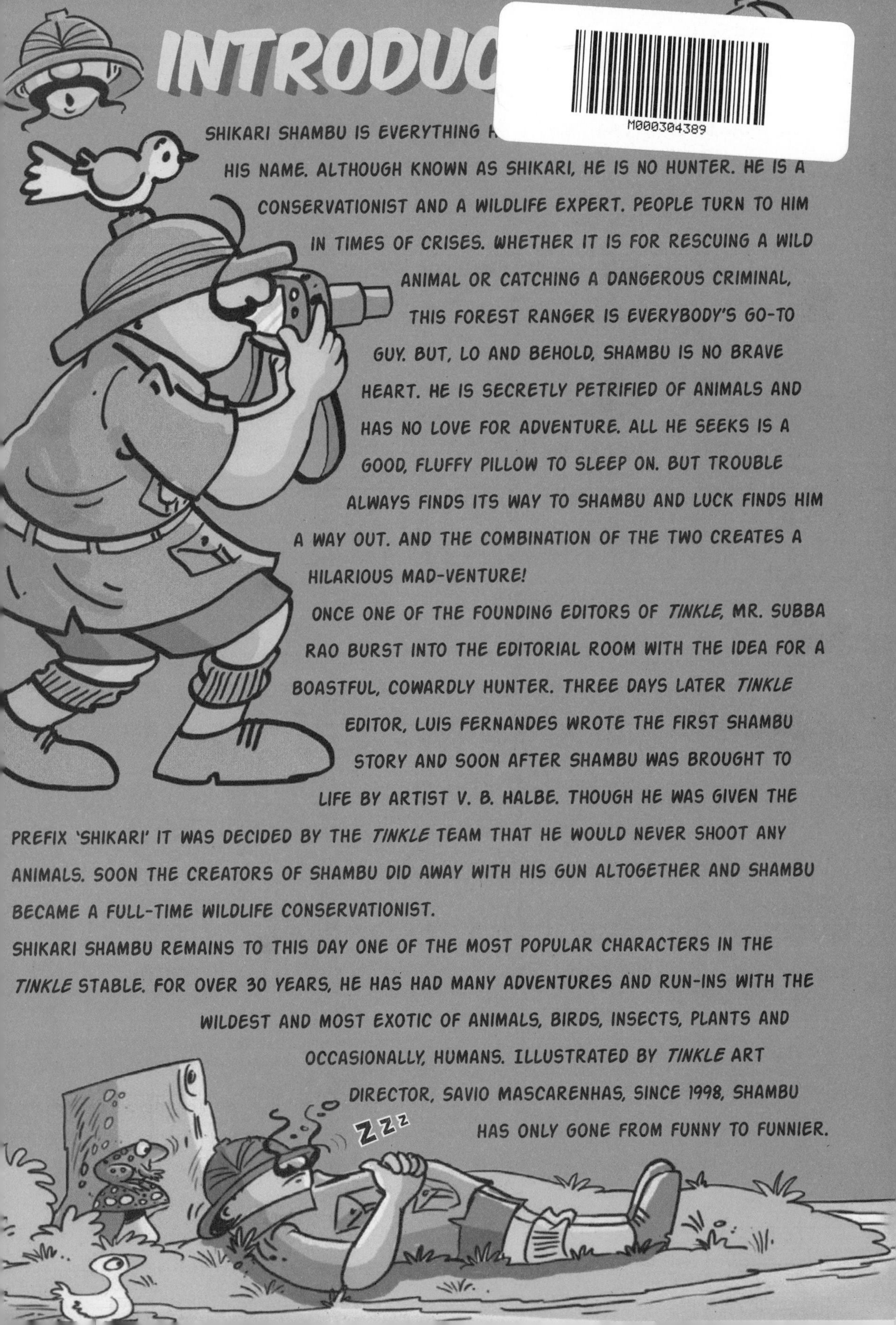

INTRODUC

SHIKARI SHAMBU IS EVERYTHING H

HIS NAME. ALTHOUGH KNOWN AS SHIKARI, HE IS NO HUNTER. HE IS A CONSERVATIONIST AND A WILDLIFE EXPERT. PEOPLE TURN TO HIM IN TIMES OF CRISES. WHETHER IT IS FOR RESCUING A WILD ANIMAL OR CATCHING A DANGEROUS CRIMINAL, THIS FOREST RANGER IS EVERYBODY'S GO-TO GUY. BUT, LO AND BEHOLD, SHAMBU IS NO BRAVE HEART. HE IS SECRETLY PETRIFIED OF ANIMALS AND HAS NO LOVE FOR ADVENTURE. ALL HE SEEKS IS A GOOD, FLUFFY PILLOW TO SLEEP ON. BUT TROUBLE ALWAYS FINDS ITS WAY TO SHAMBU AND LUCK FINDS HIM A WAY OUT. AND THE COMBINATION OF THE TWO CREATES A HILARIOUS MAD-VENTURE!

ONCE ONE OF THE FOUNDING EDITORS OF *TINKLE*, MR. SUBBA RAO BURST INTO THE EDITORIAL ROOM WITH THE IDEA FOR A BOASTFUL, COWARDLY HUNTER. THREE DAYS LATER *TINKLE* EDITOR, LUIS FERNANDES WROTE THE FIRST SHAMBU STORY AND SOON AFTER SHAMBU WAS BROUGHT TO LIFE BY ARTIST V. B. HALBE. THOUGH HE WAS GIVEN THE PREFIX 'SHIKARI' IT WAS DECIDED BY THE *TINKLE* TEAM THAT HE WOULD NEVER SHOOT ANY ANIMALS. SOON THE CREATORS OF SHAMBU DID AWAY WITH HIS GUN ALTOGETHER AND SHAMBU BECAME A FULL-TIME WILDLIFE CONSERVATIONIST.

SHIKARI SHAMBU REMAINS TO THIS DAY ONE OF THE MOST POPULAR CHARACTERS IN THE *TINKLE* STABLE. FOR OVER 30 YEARS, HE HAS HAD MANY ADVENTURES AND RUN-INS WITH THE WILDEST AND MOST EXOTIC OF ANIMALS, BIRDS, INSECTS, PLANTS AND OCCASIONALLY, HUMANS. ILLUSTRATED BY *TINKLE* ART DIRECTOR, SAVIO MASCARENHAS, SINCE 1998, SHAMBU HAS ONLY GONE FROM FUNNY TO FUNNIER.

INDEX

Shikari Shambu: Year One

Writer Sean Sequeira
Pencils & Inks Savio Mascarenhas
Colours Lidwin Mascarenhas
Letters Pranay Bendre

IT WAS THE MAASTRICHTIAN STAGE OF THE LATE CRETACEOUS PERIOD... THAT'S ABOUT 66 MILLION YEARS AGO—
THE CONTINENTS WERE DRIFTING AND THE INDIAN SUBCONTINENT WAS INCHING NORTH TO COLLIDE WITH ASIA—
INDIA
ONLY ONE MAN LIVED ON THE FLOATING INDIAN ISLAND, OUR HERO, SHAMBU—
I HOPE THE DINOSAURS CAN'T SMELL ME FROM HERE!
BUT AS ALWAYS...
SLIP
WOAH!

WHOOPS! SORRY, SORRY! PLEASE DON'T EAT ME!

THUMP

OH, NEVER MIND. YOU'RE VEGETARIAN.

SAY, COULD YOU TAKE ME A LITTLE HIGHER? I CAN ALMOST GET SOMETHING TO EAT FROM HERE! HE-HE.

SHAMBU SOON BECAME FRIENDS WITH THE HERBIVORE—

HERE, RAMU. HAVE A BITE.

BUT HERBIVORES WERE NOT THE ONLY DINOSAURS ON THE FLOATING ISLAND...

ONE DAY, SHAMBU AND RAMU WERE LOOKING FOR FOOD—
I'M TELLING YOU, RAMU. WE WILL GET SOME DELICIOUS WATERMELONS ONCE WE GET THERE.
MMM...

SUDDENLY—
GULP
ROAR
HEY! A NEW GUY! I WONDER IF HE'S FRIENDLY.

SNAP
!
AAAH! NOT FRIENDLY, NOT FRIENDLY!

??
RUN, RAMU, RUN!
POINK

WAAAAH!
WAA? HE'S CRYING? HANG ON, RAMU, LET'S SEE WHAT'S WRONG.

AH, IT'S GOT A THORN IN ITS FOOT.
POP
IT'S OUT NOW. GOODBYE, BUDDY!
COME ON, RAMU. LET'S GO GET THOSE WATERMELONS I WAS TELLING YOU ABOUT.
RAWRRRR!
WELL, WHAT DO YOU WANT NOW?
ALL RIGHT, ALL RIGHT! I LIKE YOU TOO! YOU CAN COME WITH US. I'LL CALL YOU BOBBY.
HMPH!
SLURP
COME ON, BOYS! LET'S GO LOOK FOR THAT FRUIT PLATTER.

BUT THEN—
YIKES!
ROAR
PLEASE DON'T EAT ME! PLEASE DON'T EAT ME! RUN, GUYS, RUN!
GRRR
WHERE'S BOBBY?

SNAARRLL
LOOK, RAMU! BOBBY IS PROTECTING US! FIGHT, BOBBY—PUNCH LEFT!
BLAM!
SCRATCH!
GRR
JUST THEN—
CRRRACK!
YELP!

CRRRRACK
YELP!
YIKES! OH, IT'S JUST THUNDER.
KPOW
OH NO! IT'S NOT THUNDER! THESE ARE GIANT BALLS OF FIRE! THIS CANNOT BE SAFE. QUICK! LET'S GO TO MY CAVE.
SOON—
COME ON, GUYS. GET IN!
RUMBLE RUMBLE
NO! NO! DON'T CAVE IN! MY BOYS ARE STILL OUT THERE!
KNOCK
OUCH! WHO'S THROWING ROCKS? I'M... ZZZZ...

MUCH LATER—
HOW LONG WAS I KNOCKED OUT? IS IT ALL OVER?
OH NO! SO MUCH DESTRUCTION! THE WORLD HAS ENDED. THAT MEANS...
MY BOYS! RAMU, BOBBY... (SNIFF) I'M ALL ALONE NOW!
UM... EXCUSE ME.
GASP HUH? COULD IT BE? ANOTHER HUMAN?
IS EVERYTHING OVER? IS THIS THE END?
HE-HE! NO, MISS, I THINK IT MIGHT JUST BE THE BEGINNING.

LITTLE SHAMBU: THE GHOST-CATCHER

Writer Aditya Rao | **Pencils & Inks** Savio Mascarenhas | **Colours** Umesh Sarode | **Letters** Pranay Bendre

AND SO, AT MIDNIGHT—
YIKES! WHAT DID I GET MYSELF INTO THIS TIME!
CREAAAAKKKKK!
SHAMBU WILL BE IN FOR A NASTY SURPRISE! SHAMBU, THE GHOST-CATCHER, MY FOOT!
ERRR... GUYS, WHAT'S THAT SOUND? IS THAT AN ACTUAL GHOST?
SHUT UP! THERE ARE NO SUCH THINGS AS GHOSTS!
WOOOOOOO
WOOOSSSHHH
(GULP) WHAT'S THAT THEN? I THOUGHT YOU WERE MAKING THAT SOUND!
NO, THAT'S NOT ME!
THAT MEANS... OH MY GOSH! THIS PLACE REALLY IS **HAUNTED**!
LET'S GET OUT OF HERE!
AAAAAAAAH!
MUMMYYYYYY!

DON'T EAT ME!
I'M TOO YOUNG TO DIE!
HEY, IT'S THOSE BULLIES! LOOKS LIKE THEY WERE WAITING TO FRIGHTEN ME BUT GOT SCARED THEMSELVES!
WHAT WAS I SCARED FOR? EVERYONE KNOWS THERE ARE NO SUCH THINGS AS GHOSTS. HA-HA!
MOTHER, MOTHER! I JUST SAW SHAMBU! I HEARD HE'S A DEADLY GHOST-CATCHER. I'M SO SCARED! WHAT DO WE DO?
WOOOSH
THERE, THERE, LITTLE ONE. CALM DOWN. HOW MANY TIMES HAVE I TOLD YOU? THERE ARE NO SUCH THINGS AS HUMANS!
WOOOO
THE END

REUNITED

Being separated from your best friend is the worst feeling in the world, isn't it? Then just imagine how **horrible** these Toons must be feeling, who have all been separated from their best friends! Five pairs of *Tinkle* Toon best friends have been put in different parts of a strange grid-like land. They need YOUR help to be reunited! Simply draw a path from one Toon to their best friend to connect them. The path can go in a combination of horizontal and vertical lines only. But beware! Each path you draw to connect the best friends must not overlap any other path. And after you've connected all friends, each square in the grid must have been covered. Good luck!

EXAMPLE:

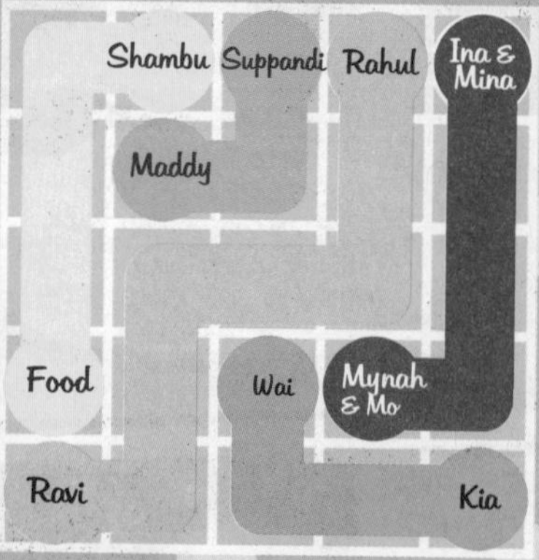

Answer on page 88

Text: Aparna Sundaresan Layout: Meera Krishnamurthy

Shikari Shambu LAB IT UP!

Story & Script Dolly Pahlajani
Pencils & Inks Savio Mascarenhas
Colours Umesh Sarode
Letters Prasad Sawant

LEKHAAA! YOU CAN'T DO ONE THING PROPERLY! AND YOU CALL YOURSELF AN EVIL SCIENTIST-IN-TRAINING?!
EVIL SCIENTISTS' SPACE RESEARCH ORGANIZATION [ESSRO].

BUT-BUT UNCLE... I—
NO 'UNCLE'! HERE I'M JUST YOUR HEAD SCIENTIST AND YOU'LL ADDRESS ME LIKE THAT!
Y-ES, PROFESSOR CHURMUR.

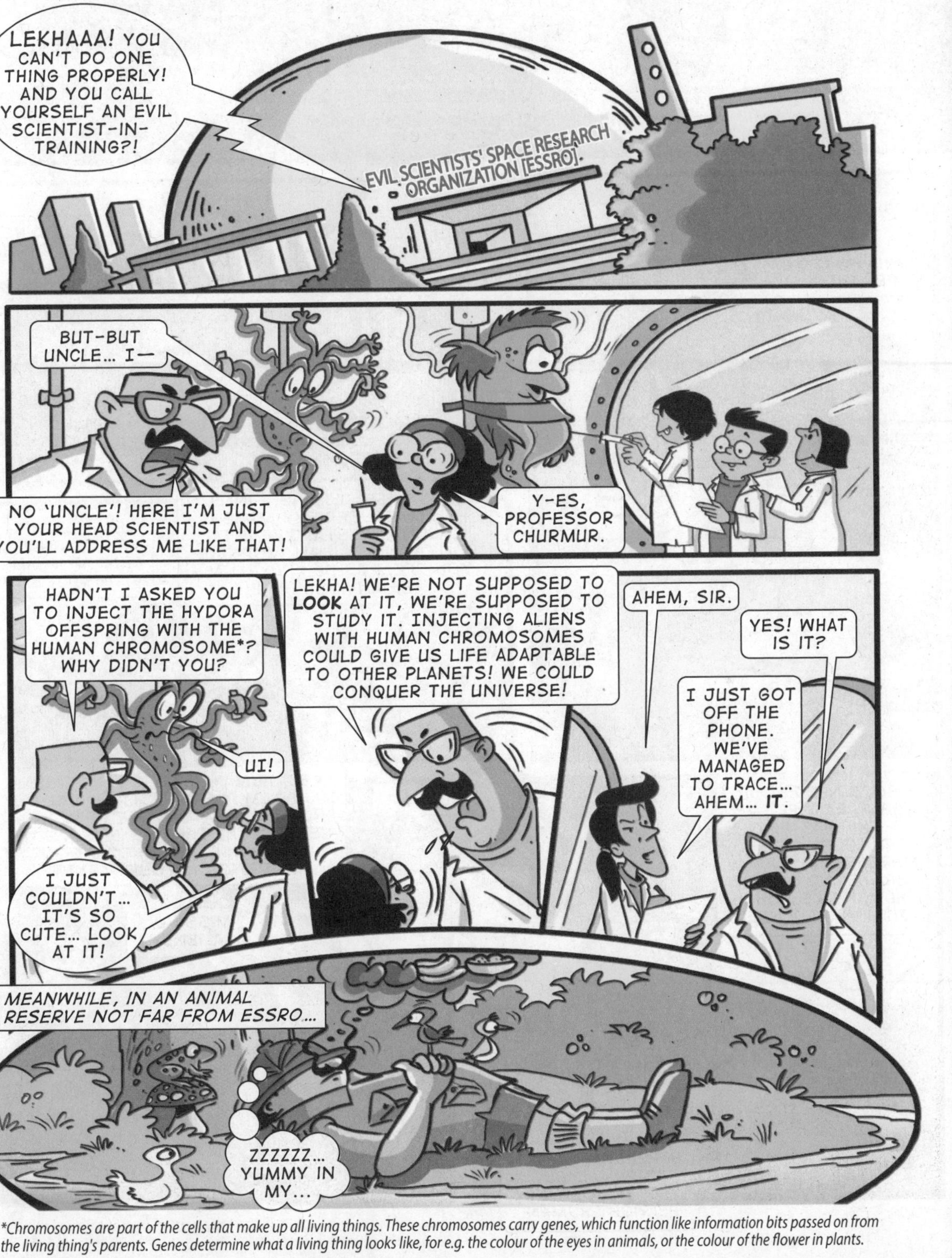

HADN'T I ASKED YOU TO INJECT THE HYDORA OFFSPRING WITH THE HUMAN CHROMOSOME*? WHY DIDN'T YOU?

UI!

I JUST COULDN'T... IT'S SO CUTE... LOOK AT IT!

LEKHA! WE'RE NOT SUPPOSED TO **LOOK** AT IT, WE'RE SUPPOSED TO STUDY IT. INJECTING ALIENS WITH HUMAN CHROMOSOMES COULD GIVE US LIFE ADAPTABLE TO OTHER PLANETS! WE COULD CONQUER THE UNIVERSE!

AHEM, SIR.

YES! WHAT IS IT?

I JUST GOT OFF THE PHONE. WE'VE MANAGED TO TRACE... AHEM... **IT**.

MEANWHILE, IN AN ANIMAL RESERVE NOT FAR FROM ESSRO...

ZZZZZZ... YUMMY IN MY...

**Chromosomes are part of the cells that make up all living things. These chromosomes carry genes, which function like information bits passed on from the living thing's parents. Genes determine what a living thing looks like, for e.g. the colour of the eyes in animals, or the colour of the flower in plants.*

...TUMMY!
OOOMPH!
WHOMP
WHA-WHO ARE YOU?!
X*#@!ZB!
WHAT ARE YOU ABUSING ME FOR?
HELLO-HELLO, MIC TESTING... 1-2-3.
AH! ENGLISH SETTING, FINALLY. HELLO, RANGER, MY NAME IS LACUNAMALISTA. I'VE BEEN FOLLOWING YOU ALL MORNING. YOU SEEM TO BE KIND TO ALL THE ANIMALS HERE.
YEAH, EXCEPT THE BIG ONES... ERM... I MEAN, YES. SO?
SO, I NEED YOUR HELP, RANGER. MY SHIP HAS GOT TANGLED IN THE MARSHES. A STRONG, BRAVE AND GENTLE HUMAN LIKE YOU IS JUST WHAT I NEED.
HEHEHEHE! DON'T WORRY, LACU. YOU'VE COME TO THE RIGHT HUMAN...
HUMAN?!
YES, HUMAN. I'M NOT, YOU SEE. I'M FROM PLANET POLICIA, FAR OUT FROM YOURS. AND I'VE BEEN SENT HERE BY THE IPF* TO INVESTIGATE SOME VISITORS WHO'VE GONE MISSING ON YOUR PLANET.
MISSING... ALIENS?!
*INTERGALACTIC POLICE FORCE

ES. IT'S REALLY SAD AND ALL THE EARTH TOURISM INDUSTRIES ARE FFERING LOSSES. HERE WE ARE... THAT'S MY SHIP.
WOAH... THAT'S—
—AARGH!
WHA-?
YOU HAVE BEEN TAKEN PRISONER BY THE EVIL SCIENTISTS' SPACE RESEARCH ORGANIZATION OF EARTH, ALIEN!
UT-BUT... I'M T AN ALIEN! I'M IKARI SHAMBU!
THE FAMOUS RANGER? EXCELLENT! EXCELLENT! YOU'VE BEEN IN TOUCH WITH THIS BEING FROM OUTER SPACE. WE'LL GET TO STUDY YOU AS WELL.
FOR NOW, REST!
WHAT DO YOU MEAN RES—
AAAAARGH!
ZZZZZ... MMM... CORN... WARM...

JUST ONE BITE... UUUNGH!
UIUIUIUIUIUIUIIIIIIII!
WHAT SCREAMED?
HUH? THIS CORN IS A LITTLE SQUISHY.
LET GO OF THE HYDORA, MISTER...
THE WHA—
YOU! YOU'RE SHIKARI SHAMBU!
UIII!
UGH! YETH, THATH ITH MNE!
I'VE READ ALL ABOUT YOU! DO YOU KNOW THERE ARE COMICS ON YOUR ESCAPADES? I'VE READ EVERY SINGLE ONE! YOU'RE MY HERO!
REALLY?
HERE, LET ME HELP YOU OUT! SUCH LUCK! I GET TO HELP MY FAVOURITE HERO! AND THAT TOO AFTER HE NARROWLY ESCAPED THE HYDORA.
HEHEHE... WHAT?
OH YEAH... THAT CREATURE WHICH WAS HUGGING YOU WITH A TENTACLE IS THE HYDORA, AN ALIEN WE CALL THE 'HUGGING STRANGLER'. THE NAME SAYS IT ALL! BUT OF COURSE, IT COULDN'T GET YOU. YOU'RE SHAMBU!
ZOOM
ER... RIGHT. OF COURSE!

WOAH! YOU MOVE FAST! PITY YOU DIDN'T ESCAPE MY UNCLE CHURMUR AND HIS TEAM. HE STARTED THIS PLACE TO EXPERIMENT ON ALIENS, SO WE CAN MAKE NEW HUMAN LIFE FORMS AND CONQUER SPACE.

SO ALL THESE ALIENS ARE LIKE HELPLESS ANIMALS IN CAGES?

ES. UNFORTUNATELY... UNLESS... **YOU** SET THEM FREE!

ME? ULP.

YES! YOU'RE SHIKARI SHAMBU. YOU HELP THE HELPLESS! AND I'LL HELP YOU!

AND I'LL SPOIL ALL MY UNCLE'S PLANS. THAT'LL SHOW HIM JUST HOW **EVIL** I CAN BE.

COME ON... LET'S GO!
BUT WHERE?!
I'M ON FOOD DUTY TODAY. WE HAVE TO DELIVER MEALS TO ALL THE ALIENS. WE'LL THINK AS WE WORK.
FOOOD! MMMM.

WE DO HAVE A DUTY TOWARDS OUR FOOD!
NO, DON'T! ALIEN FOOD HAS A TOXIC SMELL!

BUT IT'S TOO LATE. SHAMBU HAS OPENED THE LID OF ONE OF THE CONTAINERS AND—

EEWWWW! CAN'T BREATHE!

CLUNK!

BREAK GLASS IN CASE OF FIRE

SMASH

AMAZING! YOU'RE AMAZING, SHAMBU! SETTING OFF THE FIRE ALARM WILL DISABLE ALL MAINS!

AND THE ALIENS' ELECTRONIC LOCKS WILL BE DOWN FOR 10 WHOLE MINUTES. HOW DID YOU KNOW?

LUNCKY GNUESS?

SO WHILE THE WHOLE OF ESSRO WAS SCRAMBLING TO GET OUT...

EXIT

...SHAMBU AND LEKHA DID SOME RESCUING—

THAT'S THE LAST ONE!

SHAMBU, MY FRIEND! I KNEW YOU WOULD GET US OUT!

BUT YOU ARE NOT OUT YET. IT'S NOT SAFE TO LEAVE FROM THE MAIN EXITS. COME WITH ME.

IN YOU GO... THIS SEWER WILL TAKE YOU OUT OF HERE.
OH NO! DARK, DAMP, SMELLY—
FREEDOM!

YAAAA! SMELL THE FREEDOM!
YIEEEKS!

SOON—
THANK YOU, SHAMBU. YOU HAVE RESTORED OUR FAITH IN EARTHKIND. SEE YOU SOON!
ULP! I HOPE NOT.
HEAVE HO HO HO!
MEANWHILE—
LEKHAAAA! YOU DID WHAAAT?!
SET THE ALIENS FREE. PLOTTED AGAINST YOU. YOU WANTED EVIL, UNCLE. I GAVE YOU EVIL.
YES! YOU'RE EVIL. ALL MY TEST SUBJECTS! GONE!
OH! AND I DELETED ALL THE RESEARCH DATA TOO, WHILE I WAS AT IT!
NOOOOOOOO! YEARS OF RESEARCH! YEARS OF MY LIFE! WAAAAAW! YOU EVIL GIRL!
FINALLY!
FINALLY! NO MORE ALIENS. JUST MY FAMILIAR OLD BED...
...NEXT TO A SNORING WIFE AND A WARM, NEW MUFFLER... (SIGH)...ZZZZZZ
UI!

SHAMBU'S GUIDE TO GROWING TOMATOES

GROWING TOMATOES IS A GREAT WAY TO KICK-START YOUR INTEREST IN GARDENING. NOT ONLY ARE THEY EASY TO GROW, BUT THEY ALSO NEED ONLY A FEW GOOD PLANTS TO PRODUCE A LOT OF JUICY, TASTY FRUITS!

Getting started

In India, tomatoes grow in the summer and winter seasons. Choose a sunny spot in your garden or terrace as your gardening patch and ensure that the soil you use is fertile and rich in organic waste—that is, waste collected from plants and animals.

Planting the seeds

First grow seedlings by placing the seeds in some loose soil in a paper cup and sprinkling water on them every now and then until the shoots appear. You could also buy seedlings from a nursery. Plant the seedlings in the gardening patch you have prepared by placing the stem into the soil sideways and not facing up. This will ensure that your plant has a strong root system. If space is a constraint, insert a cane into the soil and tie the stem to it using a piece of cloth so that the plant grows upwards.

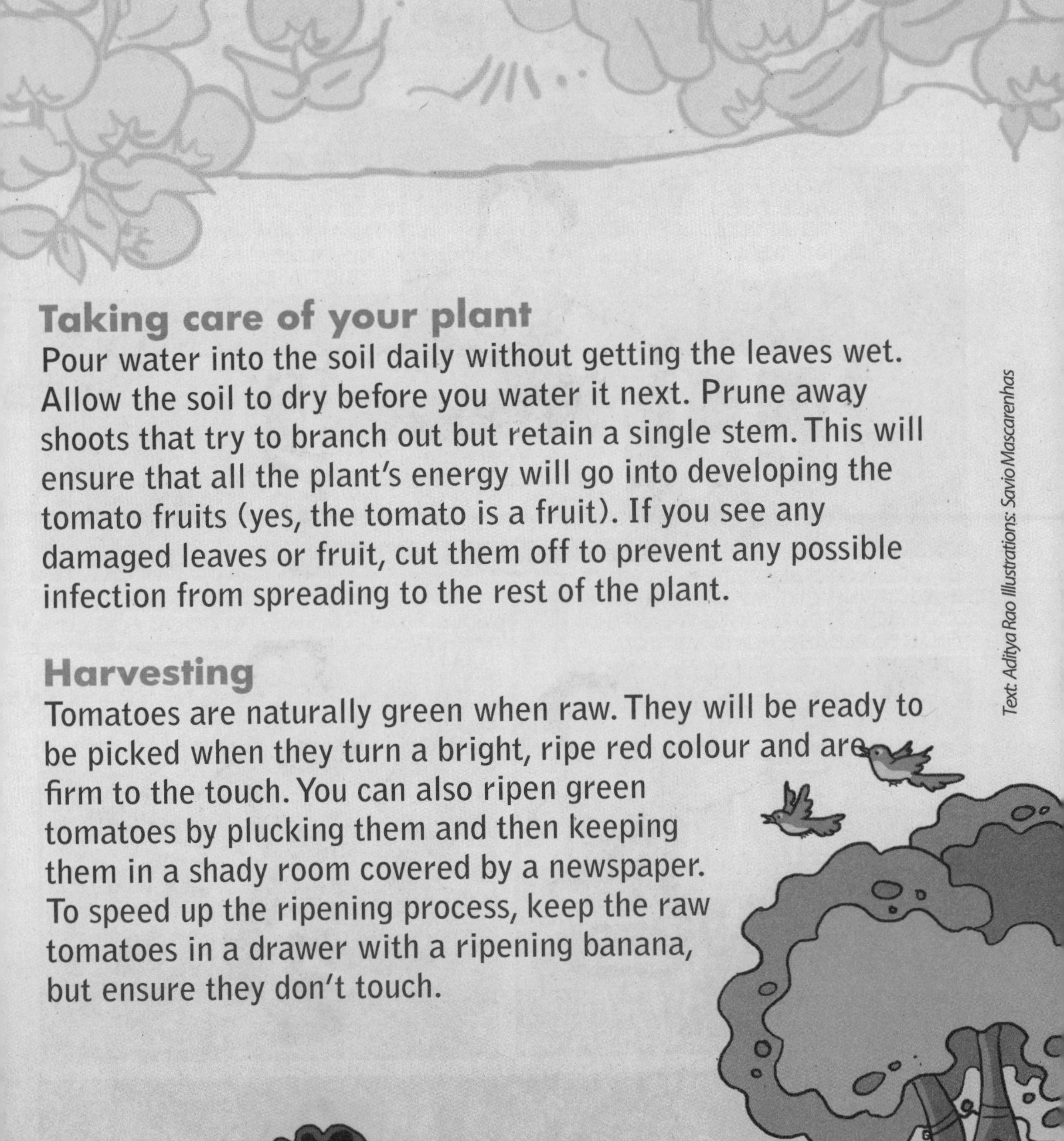

Taking care of your plant

Pour water into the soil daily without getting the leaves wet. Allow the soil to dry before you water it next. Prune away shoots that try to branch out but retain a single stem. This will ensure that all the plant's energy will go into developing the tomato fruits (yes, the tomato is a fruit). If you see any damaged leaves or fruit, cut them off to prevent any possible infection from spreading to the rest of the plant.

Harvesting

Tomatoes are naturally green when raw. They will be ready to be picked when they turn a bright, ripe red colour and are firm to the touch. You can also ripen green tomatoes by plucking them and then keeping them in a shady room covered by a newspaper. To speed up the ripening process, keep the raw tomatoes in a drawer with a ripening banana, but ensure they don't touch.

Text: Aditya Rao Illustrations: Savio Mascarenhas

SHIKARI SHAMBU: RAMBO'S VISIT

Story Multiple Writers **Script** Archita Mitra **Pencils & Inks** Savio Mascarenhas **Colours** Umesh Sarode **Letters** Prasad Sawant

SHAMBU'S SCHOOL FRIEND RAMBO WAS VISITING HIM AND SHANTI—

WOW! YOU HAVE BEEN TO AFRICA AS WELL?
YES, TO CATCH A WILD ELEPHANT THAT WAS TERRORIZING VILLAGES. CAUGHT HIM WITH MY BARE HANDS JUST LIKE THE SNOW LEOPARD IN TIBET AND THE LYNX IN FRANCE.
HA! YOU HAVEN'T CHANGED MUCH SINCE SCHOOL, RAMBO. STILL NARRATING TALL TALES.

THEY ARE NOT TALL TALES. I DON'T USE WEAPONS BUT MY BARE HANDS. I'LL DEMONSTRATE MY STRENGTH. SHANTI, PLEASE HOLD MY ARM.

OH MY, YOU ARE SO STRONG! WHAT WOULD YOU LIKE ME TO COOK FOR LUNCH?
HMPH! SHE NEVER ASKS ME WHAT I WANT FOR LUNCH!

LATER THAT DAY—
SHAMBU, MOW THE LAWN! I HAVE BEEN REMINDING YOU FOR A WEEK NOW.
WHY MOW THE LAWN WHEN THE GRASS WILL JUST GROW BACK?
HUP! LET ME DO IT, SHANTI! I WILL PULL OUT ALL THE WEEDS WITH MY BARE HANDS!
SHAMBUJI!

SHAMBUJI, WE WERE TRANSPORTING A WHITE RHINOCEROS BUT THE LOCK OF THE VAN WAS LOOSE, SO THE RHINO ESCAPED INTO THE JUNGLE. YOU MUST HELP US FIND IT!
SORRY, BUT I WON'T BE ABLE TO HELP YOU. SHANTI JUST GAVE ME A LIST OF CHORES. YOU KNOW I'M A HOUSEHOLD MAN.
OH, NOW YOU WANT TO DO THE CHORES, YOU LAZY MAN!
I WILL DO IT! I WILL ENTER THE JUNGLE AND BRING BACK THE ESCAPED RHINO. I ONLY NEED MY BARE HANDS!
SOON—
YOU ARE SUCH A COWARD! CAN'T YOU LEARN SOMETHING FROM YOUR FRIEND? HE IS SO BRAVE AND STRONG!
I AM JUST AS BRAVE AND STRONG! JUST BECAUSE I DON'T FLEX MY MUSCLES DOESN'T MEAN I'M A COWARD. I'LL CAPTURE THE WHITE RHINO BEFORE RAMBO, JUST YOU SEE!
AN HOUR LATER—
WHY IS IT ALWAYS SCARY ANIMALS THAT ESCAPE? WHY CAN'T IT BE FLUFFY RABBITS AND TIMID LAMBS?! HOW WILL I EVER CAPTURE A WHITE RHINO? BUT IF I DON'T, SHANTI WILL THINK THAT RAMBO IS STRONGER THAN ME.
OH, WHAT'S THE USE? RAMBO MUST HAVE CAPTURED THE RHINO AND RETURNED HOME BY NOW. I BET SHANTI IS PRAISING HIM AND COOKING HIM DELICIOUS KACHORIS.

I WON'T GO HOME TO SEE HER FUSSING ALL OVER HIM. I'LL JUST TAKE A NAP HERE FOR A WHILE.

MEANWHILE—
FOUND YOU! JUST YOU AND ME, OLD FELLOW. I WILL CAPTURE YOU WITH MY BARE HANDS!

FLICK
TOINK
COME ON! LET'S SEE WHAT YOU'VE GOT!

HRRRRR

AHHH!
TOING

CRASH!
OH NO, YOU DON'T! UMMPH!
HRRR
CREAK
SWISH
BACK! STAY BACK!
RUSTLE
GAAAH! HELP! EARTHQUAKE! TSUNAMI! INDIGESTION!

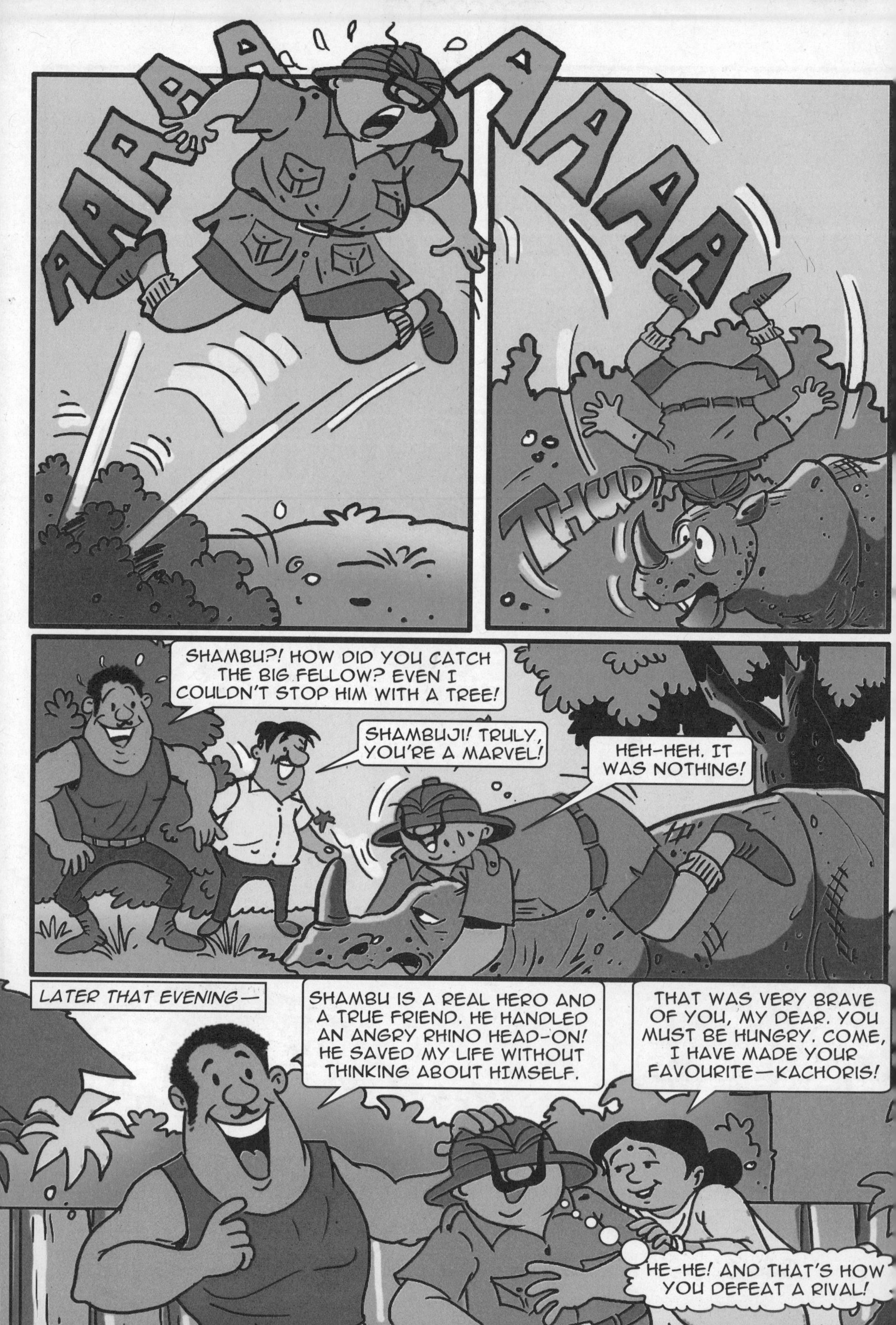

AAAAA
AAAAA
THUD!
SHAMBU?! HOW DID YOU CATCH THE BIG FELLOW? EVEN I COULDN'T STOP HIM WITH A TREE!
SHAMBUJI! TRULY, YOU'RE A MARVEL!
HEH-HEH. IT WAS NOTHING!
LATER THAT EVENING—
SHAMBU IS A REAL HERO AND A TRUE FRIEND. HE HANDLED AN ANGRY RHINO HEAD-ON! HE SAVED MY LIFE WITHOUT THINKING ABOUT HIMSELF.
THAT WAS VERY BRAVE OF YOU, MY DEAR. YOU MUST BE HUNGRY. COME, I HAVE MADE YOUR FAVOURITE—KACHORIS!
HE-HE! AND THAT'S HOW YOU DEFEAT A RIVAL!

TINKLE
YOUR FAVOURITE TINKLE TOONS WANT TO COME AND VISIT YOU!
GET BRAND NEW TINKLE ISSUES DELIVERED TO YOUR DOORSTEP EVERY FORTNIGHT!
TINKLE MAGAZINE
ANNUAL SUBSCRIPTION
24 ISSUES OF TINKLE MAGAZINE + 3 ADDITIONAL MONTHS FREE
MRP ₹960
OFFER PRICE ₹849
GET 3 EXTRA MONTHS FREE
TINKLE COMBO
ANNUAL SUBSCRIPTION
24 ISSUES OF TINKLE MAGAZINE +12 ISSUES OF TINKLE DOUBLE DIGEST
MRP ₹1800
OFFER PRICE ₹1699
PAY AN ADDITIONAL ₹300 TO RECEIVE COPIES BY COURIER
PLEASE ALLOW FOUR TO SIX WEEKS FOR YOUR SUBSCRIPTION TO BEGIN!
YOUR DETAILS
Name: Date of Birth:
Address:
City: State: Pincode:
Phone / Mobile No.:
Email:
Parent's Signature
PAYMENT OPTIONS
Cheque/DD: drawn in favour of 'ACK MEDIA DIRECT LTD.' on bank
for amount Dated: / /
SEND US YOUR COMPLETED FORM WITH YOUR CHEQUE/DD AT:
ACK MEDIA DIRECT LTD, AFL HOUSE, 7TH FLOOR, LOK BHARATI COMPLEX, MAROL-MAROSHI ROAD, ANDHERI (EAST), MUMBAI 400 059.
CUSTOMER SERVICE HELPLINE: +91-22-49188881/2 E-MAIL: CUSTOMERSERVICE@ACK-MEDIA.COM
YOU CAN ALSO LOG ON TO WWW.AMARCHITRAKATHA.COM TO SUBSCRIBE ONLINE!

Story & Script
Sean D'mello
Pencils & Inks
Savio Mascarenhas
Colours
Lidwin Mascarenhas
Letters
Pranay Bendre
LITTLE SHAMBU
DOMINOES
COME ON, DUM DUM, THE CALL OF THE WILD IS GETTING LOUDER.
YOU KNOW, I'M THE BEST STONE SKIPPER AROUND!
WOOF!
PLOP
TOING
THUD
MY HONEEYYYYY!
SPLAT

BUZZ
HONEY BEES!
THAT'S FOR TAKING OUR HONEY, FOX.
AAAAHHHHH!!
YIKES! WHAT WAS THAT SOUND?
YOU'RE GOING TO DROP THE...
...BANANAS!
THAT LITTLE BOY WILL MAKE A GREAT SNACK.

GRRR
THUMP
COME ON, DUM DUM, LET'S GO HOME.
WHOOPS!
THE OUTDOORS ARE ALWAYS FUN, BUT SOME DAYS CAN BE REALLY UNEVENTFUL.

LITTLE SHAMBU
IN DEEP WATER

Story & Script Dolly Pahlajani

Pencils & Inks Savio Mascarenhas

Colours Umesh Sarode

Letters Pranay Bendre

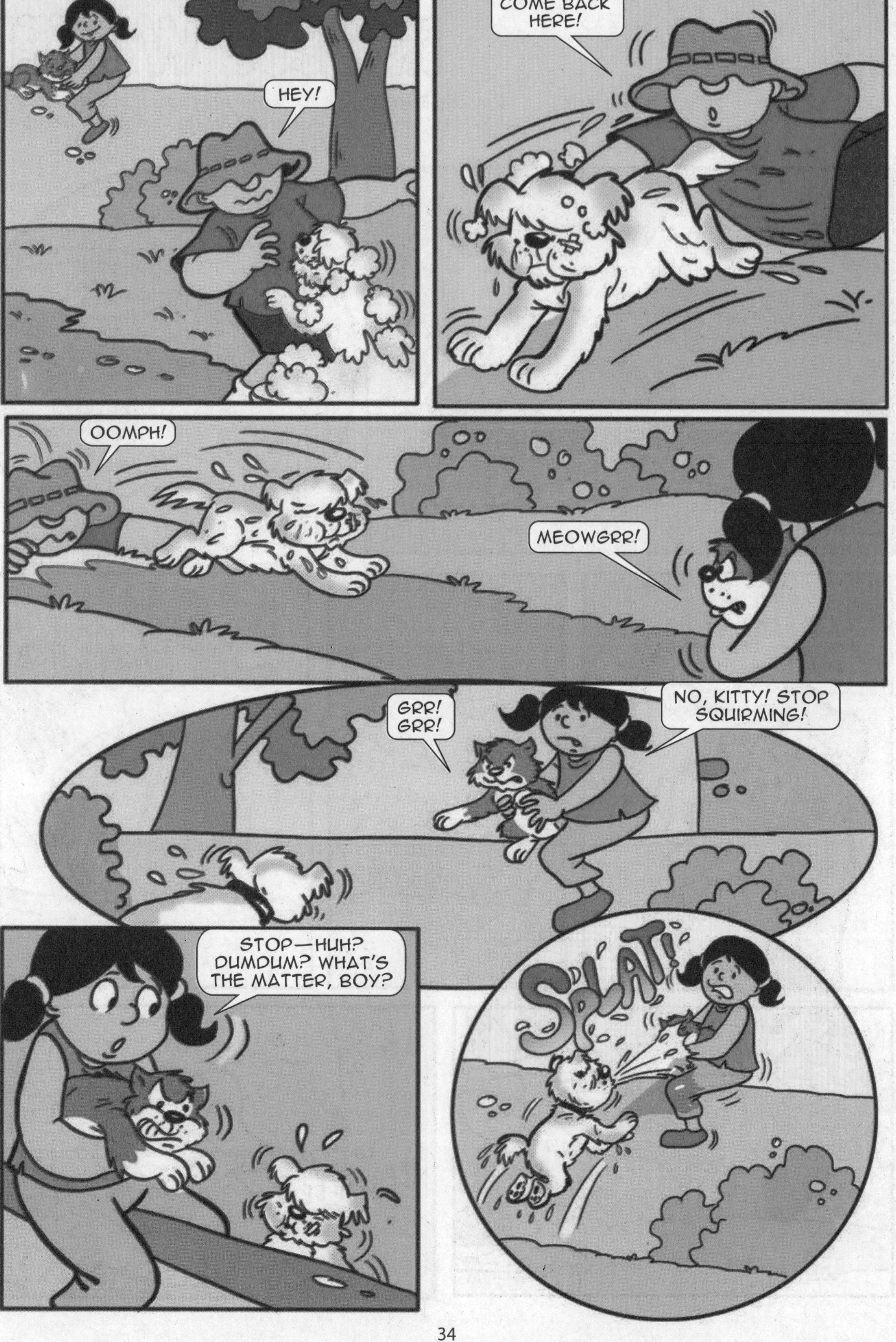
HEY!
COME BACK HERE!
OOMPH!
MEOWGRR!
NO, KITTY! STOP SQUIRMING!
GRR! GRR!
STOP—HUH? DUMDUM? WHAT'S THE MATTER, BOY?
SPLAT!

BOWHEHEHE!
GRRR!
BOW-ULP!
KITTY!
MEOW!
MEOW!
(GASP)
BOW!
DING
LEAP!
SPLASH!

SCREECH
HEHEBOW!

BOW-NA-
NA-NYA-BOW!
GRRRR.

MEOW-HMPH!

YO-BOW!!

NOT SO
FAST!

WE STILL
HAVE TO CLEAN
YOU UP!

BOW-SIGH!

WRONGFUL SCENERY

Concept & Text: Aparna Sundaresan Illustration: Savio Mascarenhas
Colours: Umesh Sarode Layout: Pranay Bendre

Ah, what a beautiful scene of the *Tinkle* Toons relaxing. But something's not right with it! Actually, four things in this scene are totally wrong! Can you figure out what they are? Circle the parts of the scene that are just impossible and cannot happen!

Answers on page 88

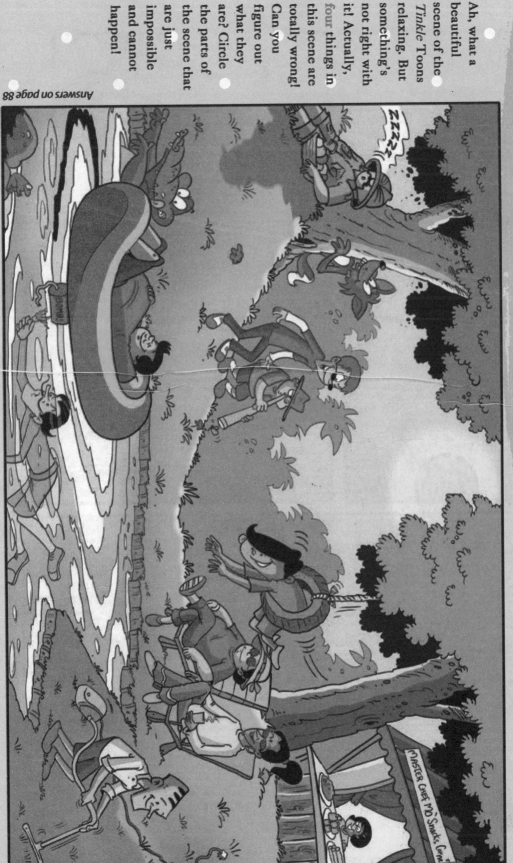

Shikari Shambu
Space Crawler
Writer
Shriya Ghate
Pencils & Inks
Savio Mascarenhas
Colours
Umesh Sarode
Letters
Pranay Bendre
SOMEWHERE IN SATURN'S ORBIT—
JUST AS I SAID, YOUR CHIEFNESS. A PEACEFUL, UNINHABITED ASTEROID.
EXCELLENT CHOICE, INTI. THIS PLACE IS IDEAL FOR MY PRIVATE GYM.

SUDDENLY—
MU-RRAAA-RRAWWW
AAAAAAAAAAAAHHHH!

YUM! SLURP! GLUG-GLUG!
RUN!!!
AAAHH!

BACK IN THEIR SPACE SHUTTLE—
...REINFORCEMENTS ARE 10,100 LIGHT YEARS AWAY, SIR. IT WILL TAKE THEM AT LEAST TWO YEARS TO GET HERE.
TWO YEARS?! I WILL HAVE YOUR HEAD FOR THIS, INTI!
I-I-I DON'T KNOW HOW I MISSED THIS... THIS... CREATURE, SIRE!
I SHOULDN'T HAVE SLEPT DURING THE SURFACE SCAN...

WE'RE DOOMED! WE'RE ALL GOING TO DIE! I WANT MY MOMMY! (SNORT)
MAYBE NOT, YOUR CHIEFNESS. THERE IS ONE WARRIOR IN THIS SOLAR SYSTEM WHO MIGHT BE ABLE TO PROTECT US.
BRING HIM TO ME!
AND SO—
MUNCH MUNCH
MMM... DELICIOUS!
ZOOOP!
WOAH!
I PRESENT TO YOU THE BRAVE AND COURAGEOUS SHAMBU! HE WILL HELP US TAKE DOWN THE CREATURE.
ALIENS?! UH-OH! I THINK I ATE THE WRONG BERRIES AGAIN. I'M IMAGINING THINGS!
WE HAVE HEARD TALES OF YOUR VALOUR. AND WE'RE HOPING YOU COULD HELP US WITH A... UMM... SMALL PROBLEM.
(GULP) YOU-YOU'VE HEARD OF **ME**?
IS THERE ANYTHING YOU NEED FROM EARTH TO FULFIL THE MISSION? WEAPONS MAYBE?

WEAPONS? OH NO, I REFRAIN FROM VIOLENCE. BUT THERE ARE A FEW THINGS... ERM... OF SUSTENANCE YOU COULD BRING ME. WRITE THIS DOWN... 30 SAMOSAS, 42 POTATO VADAS (SLURP) 57 KACHORIS...
BEEP BOOP BEEP

SEVERAL MINUTES LATER—
I'LL HAVE THESE BEAMED UP.
WAIT, WAIT! I HAVEN'T GIVEN YOU THE LIST OF DESSERTS YET!

SOON—
ARE YOU SURE THIS IS PREPARATION ENOUGH?
(CRUNCH) YES. (MUNCH) VERY GOOD!

YUM! (MUNCH MUNCH) LOW GRAVITY IS SO CONVENIENT (CHOMP) AND THIS OXYGEN MASK LETS ME EAT TOO!
GRR! IF YOU ARE WRONG ABOUT THIS MAN...
DON'T WORRY, CHIEF. THIS IS ALL PART OF HIS PROCESS. YOU'LL SEE!
I HOPE!

GRUMP
CHOMP
GUGGLE
SLURP
GRAAAAAAAAA-RRRR-AAAA!
?!?
AAAAAAAAAHHH!
ZOOP
EOWWW!
URRRRMMMP?
MRRRR-AWWW!
AAAAAAH! NO! GET AWAY FROM ME, YOU SPACE CREEPY-CRAWLEY!
COUGH COUGH
CHOMP
CHOMP
AAAARRRKKWW!
K.K. KHEERWA
MERCY! A HIDING PLACE!

UMMBRRAAAWH!
AAAAAEEEEEEEE! SPARE ME!
K K KHEERW
KNOCK

CLANG!
K.K.KHEERW
GURGLE
GURGLE

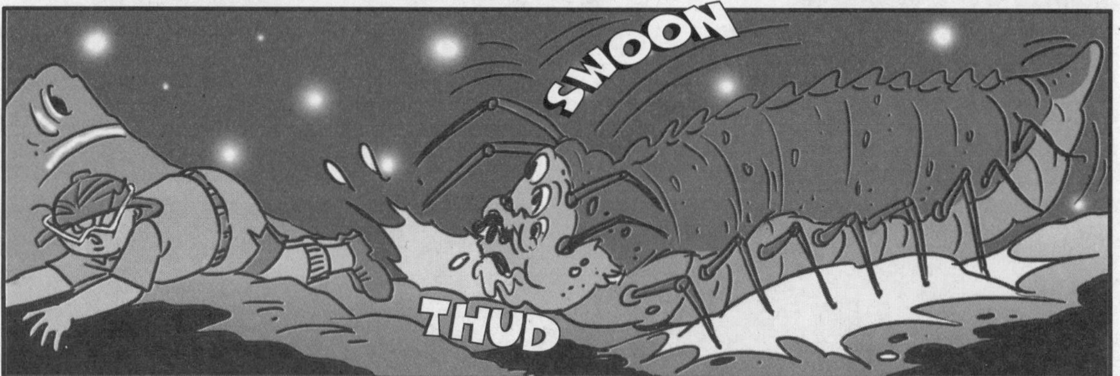
SWOON
THUD

YOU DID IT, SHAMBU! THE CREATURE IS INCAPACITATED!
MY HEAD IS SPARED!
LOOKS LIKE YOU'VE GIVEN IT A STOMACH ACHE!
STOMACH ACHE, EH? I GUESS ITS EYES ARE BIGGER THAN ITS BELLY! HE-HE!

YIPEE! NOW I CAN BUILD MY PRIVATE GYM!
SHAMBU, YOU ARE EVERY BIT THE WARRIOR I HEARD OF. TELL ME WHAT YOU WISH FOR AND IT'S YOURS!
WELL, AS MUCH AS I LOVED BEING ON THIS... UMM... DELIGHTFUL ASTEROID OF YOURS, I WOULD LIKE TO RETURN TO EARTH NOW.

AND SO—
YOU'RE TELLING ME YOU TRAV-ELLED ALL THE WAY TO AN ASTEROID NEAR SATURN AND BROUGHT DOWN A GIANT SPACE CRAWLER? PAH! YOU DON'T HAVE THE HEART FOR IT!
(SLURP) BUT I DEFINITELY HAVE THE STOMACH FOR IT! HE-HE-HE!
?

SHAMBU'S WILD SHOTS

Chestnut Blight

Script: Dolly Pahlajani

Art & Letters: Savio Mascarenhas

WHOA! WHAT A LOVELY SPOT FOR A NAP!

THAT'S A PHOTO OF MY GRANDPA SLEEPING UNDER THE FAMOUS AMERICAN CHESTNUT TREE.

"THE AMERICAN CHESTNUT WAS ONE OF THE MOST COMMONLY-FOUND TREES IN ITS NATIVE, NORTH-EASTERN UNITED STATES, AND MADE UP 25 TO 30 PER CENT OF ITS FOREST.

THIS IS NUTS! WHY CAN'T I REACH IT?!

"THESE TREES WERE HUGE—ABOUT 30.5 METRES TALL AND 7 METRES AROUND. HUMANS LOOKED LIKE DWARFS BEFORE THEM.

THEIR ROT-RESISTANT WOOD WAS USED TO MAKE EVERYTHING FROM HOUSES AND FURNITURE TO SHIPS AND MUSICAL INSTRUMENTS.

"THEIR PROTEIN-PACKED CHESTNUTS WERE A STAPLE FOR MANY FAMILIES.

"THE PROBLEM STARTED BETWEEN THE LATE 1800S AND EARLY 1900S—

HERE IS THE NEW ASIAN CHESTNUT IMPORTED FROM JAPAN. IT WILL ADD TO THE BEAUTY OF OUR FORESTS.

"WHAT THESE PEOPLE DIDN'T KNOW WAS THAT THE ASIAN CHESTNUT HARBOURED A FUNGUS* IN ITS BARK.

YEAH, FOLKS! WE'RE FINALLY IN AMERICA!
LET'S GO SEE WHICH NEW TREES WE CAN EAT!

"THE ASIAN CHESTNUT HAD BEEN EXPOSED TO THIS FUNGUS A LOT IN JAPAN, AND SO, WAS RESISTANT TO IT.

*The fungus is called *Cryphonectria parasitica* (formerly *Endothia parasitica*)

"BUT THE AMERICAN CHESTNUT WAS UNPREPARED FOR AN ATTACK ON ITS HOME TURF.
AH! YUM! THIS TREE IS AMAZINGLY TASTY!
YES! LET'S CHECK OUT MORE OF ITS KIND.
"THE FUNGUS ATTACKED IT, AND ITS DEFENCES WERE USELESS AGAINST THE FOREIGN ORGANISM.

"THE WIND SPREAD THE VIRUS FAR AND WIDE AND SO DID UNSUSPECTING CREATURES WHICH HAD BEEN IN CONTACT WITH AN INFECTED TREE.

TAK-TAK-TAK
HEY, THANKS FOR THE RIDE, BRO!

"WITHIN 40 YEARS, THERE WERE NO CHESTNUT TREES LEFT. THEY HAD ALL BEEN INFECTED, WEAKENED AND WITHERED TO NOTHING.

"BUT THERE ARE SOME SURVIVORS—NOT FULLY-GROWN TREES LIKE BEFORE, BUT YOUNG ONES. THEY ARE PROTECTED FROM THE FUNGUS.

"SEE, THIS ONE HERE HAS BEEN FENCED IN BY WIRES SO THAT DEER DON'T CREATE CRACKS IN THE BARK WITH THEIR ANTLERS. THESE CRACKS COULD ALLOW THE FUNGUS TO ENTER THE TREE.

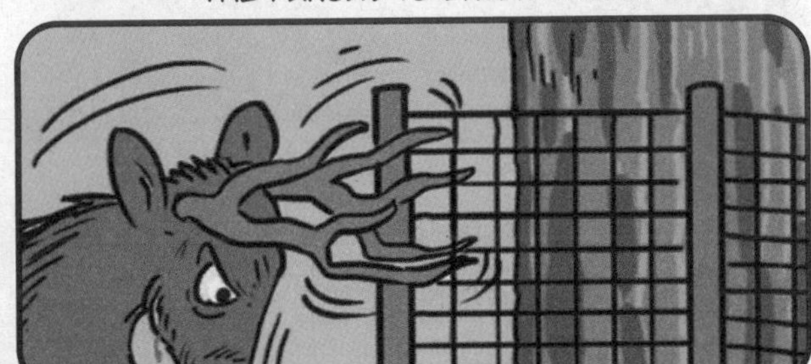

"MOREOVER, SCIENTISTS ARE NOW TRYING TO BREED A HYBRID OF THE AMERICAN CHESTNUT AND THE MORE FUNGUS-RESISTANT ASIAN CHESTNUT TREES."

I HOPE THE AMERICAN CHESTNUT COMES BACK SOON. I HAVE HEARD SO MUCH ABOUT ITS YUMMY NUTS THAT I'M EAGER TO TRY THEM!

SHIKARI SHAMBU
AT THE EDGE OF THE WORLD
Story & Script
Shruti Dave
Pencils & Inks
Savio Mascarenhas
Colours
Umesh Sarode
Letters
Pranay Bendre
TWO DAYS AGO—
SHAMBU SIR, HOW ARE YOU PLANNING TO CELEBRATE THIS WORLD ENVIRONMENT DAY? ANY SPECIAL MISSIONS?
I'M GOING TO NEW ZEALAND ON A PERSONAL MISSION TO DEEPEN MY BOND WITH NATURE...
...WHERE NO ONE WILL DISTURB MY SLUMBER. HEE-HEE.
TODAY—
SNORE
SNOOOREE UHRM...
SO, YOU ARE FINALLY AWAKE.
AAARGH! W-WHO ARE YOU? WHY AM I IN THE MIDDLE OF THE OCEAN?!
YOU HAVE NOTHING TO BE AFRAID OF. THOUGH I'VE HEARD THE GREAT SHIKARI SHAMBU NEVER IS.
I HATE MY REPUTATION. SOMETIMES.
AHOY, SKIPPER!
YOU, SHAMBU SIR, ARE IN THE RIGHT PLACE.
UNLESS YOU'VE GOT FOOD HERE, I CAN'T AGREE WITH YOU.

*A DESSERT FAMOUS IN NEW ZEALAND

GUYS! THE SHIPS ARE HERE!
SHIPS? HOW MANY?
THREE! AND THEY'RE *BIG*!
WHAT DO YOU THINK OUR STRATEGY SHOULD BE, SHAMBU?
MAYBE WE SHOULD FIND OUT FIRST IF THEY ARE REALLY HERE TO HUNT WHALES...
...IF NOT, THEN I CAN GO HOME!
A DIRECT CONFRONTATION! RIGHT THEN. LET'S GET CLOSER TO THEM! MOVE!
CLOSER?! THAT'S NOT WHAT I MEANT...
ALERT! THIS IS A WHALE SANCTUARY. TELL US YOUR PURPOSE FOR BEING HERE.
WE ARE HERE FOR A SCIENTIFIC RESEARCH PROJECT. KINDLY GIVE US WAY.
HA! THEY REALLY THINK WE'RE GOING TO BELIEVE THAT? SEND A DRONE OVER THEIR HEADS!
AYE, AYE, CAPTAIN!
WHY DO I HAVE A FEELING THINGS ARE GOING TO GET REAL BAD REAL SOON...
I SEE IT! I SEE THEIR HUNTING EQUIPMENT.
WE SEE YOUR HUNTING EQUIPMENT. BACK AWAY NOW. WHALING IS ILLEGAL!

GET OUT OF OUR WAY. **WE REPEAT.** WE ARE HERE FOR SCIENTIFIC RESEARCH ONLY!
WHAT DO WE DO, SHAMBU?
WE CAN'T BACK OFF HERE, WE...

YOU'RE RIGHT! NO BACKING AWAY! WE STAY AND PROTECT!
YAYYY!
YAYYY!
YAYYY!

NO, NO! I MEANT THERE'S AN ICEBERG BEHIND US. WE'VE GOT NOWHERE TO GO!

WE WILL NOT BACK AWAY! WE REPEAT. LEAVE NOW OR YOU'LL HAVE TO GO THROUGH **US**!
US? YOU MEAN ME INCLUDED?

ERM, SID. I THINK THEY'RE MOVING TOWARDS US.

THEN WE MOVE FORWARD! **GO!**

THUD!

OH NO! WE'RE GOING TO CRASH INTO THE ICEBERG. THE MAST IS GOING TO FALL!
CRACK
CRASH!
WOOO! SLIPPERY-VIPPERY DECK!
I'D BETTER GET THIS ICE OUT OF THE WAY BEFORE I SLIP AND FALL INTO THE SEA!
UH...
TWACK!
...OH.
CRASH!

SHAMBU! THAT WAS GREAT!
REALLY? I MEAN, OF COURSE IT WAS!
EVERYBODY! CATAPULT THE ICE CHUNKS AND AIM FOR THEIR MAST, LIKE SHAMBU DID!
TENNIS BALL SHOOTER
ZOOP
LOOK! THEY'RE BACKING AWAY! WE'VE DONE IT!
YOU'VE DONE IT, SHAMBU! WE'VE SAVED THE WHALES!
YAYY! HURRAYY!
AFTER MANY DAYS—
SHAMBU SIR, YOUR FIGHT AGAINST THE WHALERS WAS CAPTURED ON CAMERA BY YOUR SHIP'S DRONE AND SEEN BY EVERYONE. YOU'RE A WORLDWIDE HERO!
THANK YOU.
ONE LAST QUESTION, SIR—WERE YOU OT SCARED DURING THE MISSION?
GAK!
SWOOOSH
WHALELY... I MEAN, HARDLY! HEE-HEE!
SPLASH

CUPCAKE CATASTROPHE

Someone has eaten all the cupcakes at the annual *Tinkle* birthday bash! Shanti is furious. She spent all day making those cupcakes for all the *Tinkle* Toons. She thinks Shikari Shambu is the one who's eaten them all. Shambu pleads his innocence. He insists he's been at his table eating soup for the last 10 minutes, so it couldn't have been him! However, Shanti doesn't believe him. Help Shambu find out just why Shanti doesn't buy his flimsy excuse.

Answer on page 88

Text: Sean D'mello Illustration: Abhijeet Kini Studios Layout: Pranay Bendre

hikari Shambu & Mopes & Purr:
layhem on the Mountain
Writer
Dushyant S.
Pencils & Inks
Savio Mascarenhas
Colours
Lidwin Mascarenhas
Letters
Prasad Sawant
ONE MORNING IN THE HIMALAYAS—
GASP! MY FLOCK! WHAT COULD HAVE HAPPENED?
SNOW LEOPARD!
OH NO! YETI!
AAAAAA!
MEANWHILE, AN IMPORTANT HOLIDAY MAKER ARRIVED—
ADGHAR
TATION
AAAH! THE FRESH MOUNTAIN AIR! JUST WHAT I NEED TO REJUVENATE MYSELF WHILE SHANTI REJU-VENATES WITHOUT ME.
PREPAID TAXI AVAILABLE

MEANWHILE, IN MUMBAI—
GOSH, THINGS HAVE BEEN REALLY SLOW AROUND HERE!
YOU'RE RIGHT. EVEN DABOO SEEMS TO HAVE VANISHED FROM THE CRIME SCENE. MAYBE WE COULD TAKE A SMALL VACATION.
I SPY & WHY
SO BAGS PACKED, MOPES AND PURR SET OFF—
SO MOPES, WHAT'S OUR HOLIDAY ITINERARY?
MY COUSIN, PAHADI, WORKS AS A SHEEPDOG IN THE MOUNTAINS. HE'S PROMISED US A WEEKEND OF SKIING!
MOPES! PURR! I'M SO GLAD YOU COULD MAKE IT. THINGS HAVE BEEN REALLY STRANGE AROUND HERE AND WE SURE COULD USE THE HELP OF SOME ACE DETECTIVES!
WELL, THIS WASN'T THE RECEPTION WE WERE EXPECTING! WE'RE SUP-POSED TO BE ON HOLIDAY!
TAXI BOOKING COUNTER
BUT NO WORRIES. WE'D BE HAPPY TO HELP!
SHAMBU'S TRIP WAS ALSO NOT GOING AS PLANNED—
MY GOOD FELLOW, DO YOU MEAN TO TELL ME THAT MUTTON IS ENTIRELY OFF THE MENU?
THE LOCAL GOATHERDS KEEP LOSING ANIMALS TO SOME INTRUDER. THEY CAN'T PROVIDE THE STOCK WE NEED.

SHAMBU DECIDED TO TACKLE THE PROBLEM AT ITS SOURCE—
NOW, COULD YOU ALL EXPLAIN TO ME EXACTLY WHAT'S BEEN GOING ON WITH THE GOATS?

GONE! ALL GONE!
THEY COME AT NIGHT!
WORK OF A SNOW LEOPARD!
WITH FANGS LIKE KNIVES!
NOT A LEOPARD, THE YETI!

ALL RIGHT, THANK YOU. BUT YETIS ARE NOT REAL. THE SNOW LEOPARD, HOWEVER, I SHALL SEE TO.

AND I PRAY THAT THE SNOW LEOPARD IS JUST AS IMAGINARY!

AND SO SHAMBU'S GETAWAY TURNED INTO A WORKING VACATION—
(GASP) (HUFF)
WHY DON'T I EVER LEARN MY LESSON AND JUST KEEP MUM?!

HOURS LATER—
UH-OH, IT'S GETTING DARK. MUTTON OR NO MUTTON, THE HOTEL SOUNDS LIKE A GOOD IDEA.

UNBEKNOWNST TO SHAMBU, THE SNOW LEOPARD'S DEN WAS RIGHT AROUND THE NEXT BEND—
(SNIFF SNIFF) I SMELL HUMAN...
GRRR
RAAARRRR
AAAH!

MEANWHILE, MOPES AND PURR WERE CONDUCTING THEIR INVESTIGATION—
THESE GUYS WILL TELL YOU WHAT'S BEEN HAPPENING AROUND HERE.

THE HUMANS DON'T GUARD US BECAUSE
HEY'RE SCARED OF THE PREDATORS AND MONSTERS THAT THEY THINK ARE ATTACKING US, BUT THEY'RE WRONG!
IT'S THIS INFERNAL PACK OF DOGS! THEY MAKE FAKE FOOTPRINTS ON THE SNOW TO FOOL EVERYONE. AND THEIR BOSS IS THIS HORRIBLE DOG THAT BAAA-BARKS AT EVERYONE!
OUND FAMILIAR, PURR?
JUST LIKE OUR OLD FRIEND—
DID YOU MISS ME?
GET 'EM, BOYS!
DABOO! YOU'RE NOT GOING TO GET AWAY WITH THIS!

OH, BUT I AM! AND I'M GOING TO TURN ALL YOUR PRECIOUS GOATS INTO LEATHER! HA-HA-HA!
GRRR

JUST THEN—
COMING THROUGH!

THUD!
OUCH!

RAAARRR
RUN FOR YOUR LIVES!
ULP

G-GOOD KITTY, S-SWEET KITTY. D-DOES KITTY WANT MILK?
THAT'S IT. HE'S DONE FOR!

OOH! I CAN'T WATCH!

BUT THEN—
YEOWWW!

THAT'S RIGHT! DON'T YOU EVER COME BACK!

JOB WELL DONE, SHAMBU OLD CHAP! HE-HE-HE!

ANOTHER PROBLEM SOLVED! AND NOW I'M OFF!

LOOKS LIKE WE'VE FOILED YOUR PLANS AGAIN, DABOO.
THIS TIME WITH A LITTLE HELP FROM THE FAMOUS SHIKARI SHAMBU!
PHOOEY! IF THAT LEOPARD HADN'T BEEN SCARED OFF, I WOULD HAVE BEEN FREE!

AND WHAT, OR WHO, EXACTLY SCARED THE SNOW LEOPARD OFF? OUR HEROES WILL NEVER KNOW THE TRUTH...

SSSHHH!

...BUT WE WILL!

TERRIFIC TINKLE COLLECTIONS
JUST A CLICK AWAY

Tinkle Assorted Double Digests
(Pack of 24)
₹2669

Tinkle Assorted Digests
(Pack of 24)
₹1649

Tinkle Assorted Digests
(Pack of 50)
₹3459

Best of Tinkle Assorted Double Digests
(Pack of 5)
₹600

Best of Tinkle Assorted Double Digests
(Pack of 10)
₹1199

Tantri the Mantri-The Essential Collection
(Pack of 7)
₹875

Tinkle Celebrations Pack 1
₹699

Tinkle Celebrations Pack 2
₹899

Tinkle Celebrations Pack 3
₹1199

FAST SELLING

(Vol. 1)

(Vol. 2)

(Vol. 3)

Tinkle Origins
₹349 (each)

Adventures with Shambu
(Pack of 7)
₹875

Tinkle Special Collection-Vol 1
(Pack of 3)
₹349

Tinkle Special Collection-Vol 2
(Pack of 3)
₹349

Tinkle Special Collection-Vol 3
(Pack of 3)
₹349

Tinkle Special Collection-Vol 4
(Pack of 3)
₹349

Tinkle Special Collection-Vol 5
(Pack of 3)
₹349

Tinkle Special Collection-Vol 6
(Pack of 3)
₹349

Superstars of Tinkle
(Pack of 17)
₹1999

Folktales from Around The World
(Pack of 4)
₹450

Tinkle Folktales from Around The World
(Pack of 9)
₹999

BEST SELLING

Suppandi-The Essential Collection
(Pack of 9)
₹1199

LOG ON TO **WWW.AMARCHITRAKATHA.COM**
OR CALL US AT **022 4918 888 1/2** TO PLACE YOUR ORDER TODAY!

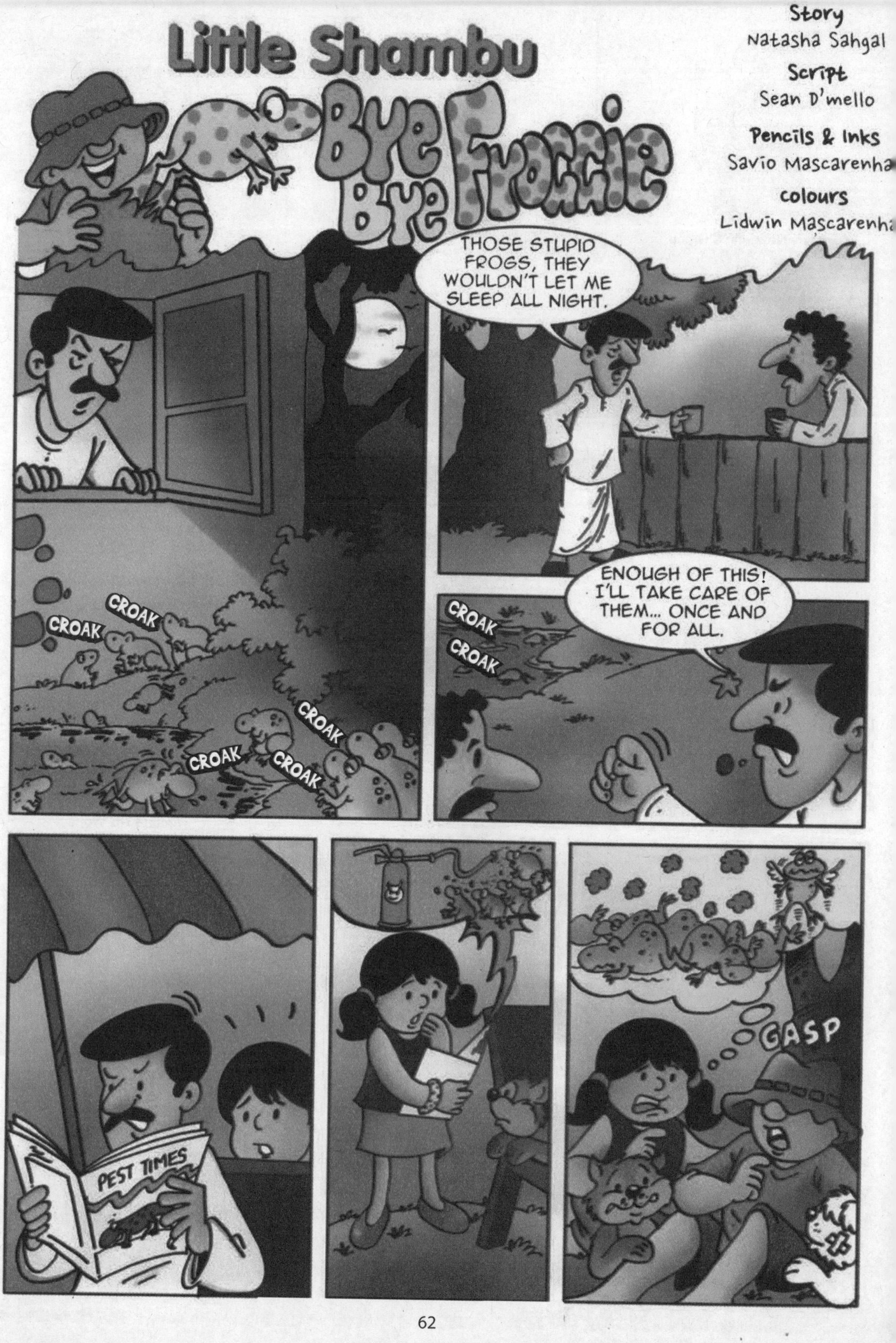

Little Shambu

Bye Bye Froggie

Story
Natasha Sahgal
Script
Sean D'mello
Pencils & Inks
Savio Mascarenha
colours
Lidwin Mascarenha

CROAK
CROAK
CROAK
CROAK
CROAK

THOSE STUPID FROGS, THEY WOULDN'T LET ME SLEEP ALL NIGHT.

CROAK
CROAK

ENOUGH OF THIS! I'LL TAKE CARE OF THEM... ONCE AND FOR ALL.

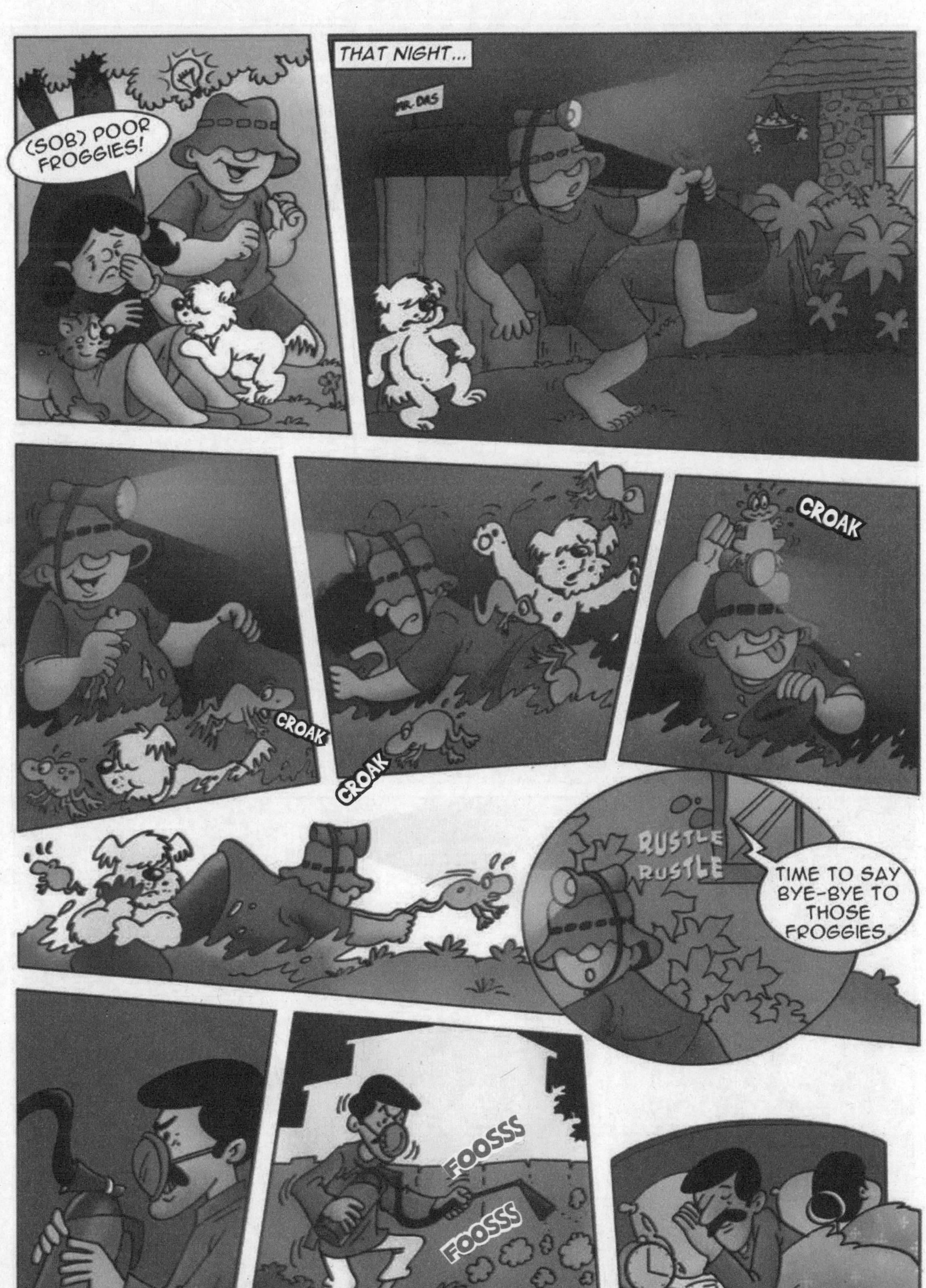

(SOB) POOR FROGGIES!
THAT NIGHT...
MR. DAS
CROAK
CROAK
CROAK
RUSTLE
RUSTLE
TIME TO SAY BYE-BYE TO THOSE FROGGIES.
FOOSSS
FOOSSS

THE NEXT MORNING...
APRIL 10
MOM, DAD, MOSQUITOES BIT ME THROUGHOUT THE NIGHT.

AT THE NEIGHBOURS', A SIMILAR STORY UNFOLDED.
APRIL 13

AARGH, STUPID MOSQUITOES. THEY'VE GOTTEN TO ALL OF US!
SWAT

RIGHT THERE, THAT'S THE SPOT.

DON'T TELL ME THOSE MOSQUITOES GOT TO YOU TOO.
I WONDER WHERE THIS SWARM OF MOSQUITOES CAME FROM.

MAYBE WE SHOULD CALL A DOCTOR.
I'M WORRIED ABOUT THE KIDS. HOW IS LITTLE SHAMBU DOING?

HE'S...
...FINE?!
HOW?

?!! ??
I'VE GOT A SECRET MOSQUITO REPELLENT, ONE YOU ALL GAVE UP ON. COME, I'LL SHOW YOU!

CROAK
CROAK
CROAK

SHIKARI SHAMBU BEST OF BOTH WORLDS
Story Concept
Sagar Venkateshwar
Story & Script
Dolly Pahlajani
Pencils & Inks
Savio Mascarenhas
Colours & Letters
Lidwin Mascarenhas
COME BACK HERE WITH MY LUNCHBOX, YOU!
HAAHAAHEEHEE
IT MAYBE A HYENA (GASP), BUT IT SURE RUNS LIKE A CHEETAH (PUFF). OH DEAR (HUFF)! MAYBE I SHOULD SAY MY LAST GOODBYES TO THE FOOD.
CLICK!
SHANTI'S FAMOUS GOBI PARATHAS WITH (SNIFF-SNIFF) LEMON PICKLE.
SNIFF-SNIFF
I CAN'T LET THEM GO.
I SHALL FOLLOW YOU TO THE ENDS OF THE GOBI DESERT FOR THOSE GOBI PARATHAS, HYENA!
YAAAAAAOOOO NOOOOOOO! I'M GOING TO HIT THE TREE!
HAAHAAHEEHEE!
POOF!

AAAAAAAAAAAA!
ZOOOP
THUD!
WELCOME TO MY HUMBLE ABODE.
HUH?!
WOW! I TOLD MY WIFE TO FIND SOMEONE JUST LIKE ME AND SHE DID!
YEAH, SHE'S MY WIFE, SHANTI. AND I'M SHIKARI SHAMBU.
YOUR WIFE?

BU-BUT... THAT'S **MY** NAME! AND MY WIFE IS NAMED SHANTI TOO... ALTHOUGH SHE'S NOT A HYENA. STILL, SHE DOES LAUGH AT ME A LOT.
AH, YOU LOOK LIKE ME, YOUR WIFE IS LIKE MY WIFE AND WE EVEN HAVE THE SAME NAME! WHICH MEANS...
...IT WAS MEANT TO BE! WE WERE MEANT TO FIGHT EVIL TOGETHER... TWO BRAVE SHIKARIS.
THIS SOUNDS LIKE A BAD DREAM. I HOPE WAKE UP SOON
COME, LET ME SHOW YOU WHY I ASKED FOR HELP FROM THE OUTSIDE WORLD.
OUTSIDE WORLD? Y-YOU MEAN... WE'RE NOT ON EARTH?
UH... WE ARE ON EARTH... JUST NOT YOUR EARTH. THIS IS MY EARTH. THEY KIND OF EXIST LIKE TWO BRANCHES OF THE SAME TREE. THE TREE THAT YOU CAME THROUGH, IN FACT.
OH DEAR... I DIDN'T KNOW DREAMS COULD BE SO COMPLICATED. MY HEAD HURTS.
FORGET ALL THAT... AND LOOK HERE. THE PEOPLE OF MY SETTLEMENT HAVE ASSEMBLED TO GREET YOU.
PEOPLE? BUT THEY'RE ANIMALS!
THEY ARE NOW. BUT THEY USED TO BE PEOPLE. SOMETHING CHANGED THEM ALL.
I AM THE ONLY ONE LEFT. AND I MAY TURN TOO UNLESS WE FIND THE SOURCE OF THE TROUBLE AND DESTROY IT.
ULP... **WE**?

YES... WE WILL NOT WATCH THE WORLD ROUND US TURN UPSIDE DOWN. IT'S DO OR DIE!
D-D-DIE?
I DON'T WANT TO DIEEEEEEE! TREE PORTAL, HERE I COMEEEEEE!
WELL-WELL... SO MUCH ENTHUSIASM TO FACE DANGER! HE CERTAINLY IS LIKE ME!
HEY, WAIT UP. I'M COMING TOO!
(GASP-PUFF) WHICH TREE WAS IT... THEY ALL LOOK THE SAME!
WHAT ARE YOU LOOKING FOR? DID YOU SENSE SOMETHING UNUSUAL?
UH... I-UH... WATER! I'M LOOKING FOR WATER.
WELL, IN THAT CASE, LET ME LEAD YOU TO THE SPRING.
GREAT! HOW DO I SPRING OUT OF THIS NOW?
THERE IT IS—WAIT... THAT DOESN'T LOOK RIGHT.
YOU MEAN RED BUBBLING SPRINGS ARE NOT NORMAL ON YOUR EARTH TOO? THAT'S A RELIEF!
OI! YOU THERE— MONKEY! DON'T DRINK THAT WATER! IT DOES NOT LOOK SAFE!
!

HEY, LET'S FOLLOW THAT MONKEY!
LIKE I HAVE A CHOICE!
OOO O OOO!!
GO ON... I'M RIGHT BEHIND YOU.
(SIGH) I WISH I COULD JUST 'LOG' OUT OF THIS MONKEY BUSINESS.
WHAT IS THIS PLACE? LOOKS LIKE A LAB OF SOME KI—
OO!
OOO O OOO!!
YIEEKES!
WHAT'S GOING ON?!
YAAAAAA!
SPLASH!
BAM!

WHAT'S GOING ON? WHO IS THIS VICIOUS MONKEY?
(COUGH-COUGH -SPUTTER!)
OO-AA-AA! I AM A FAMOUS HUMAN SCIENTIST, OKAY? AND I'M AN ORANGUTAN NOW, NOT A MONKEY, YOU IGNORAMUS.
RIIIGHT. AND WHY ARE YOU AN ORANGUTAN? SCIENCE CAUSED REVERSE EVOLUTION?
NO. I WAS JUST TIRED OF THE DAILY RIND AND DECIDED THAT AN ANIMAL HAS SUCH AN EASY LIFE. NO PRESSURES OF EW INVENTIONS, JUST FOOD AND PEACE OF MIND. SO I MADE MYSELF A SERUM THAT'D TURN ME INTO AN ANIMAL.
BUT HOW COULD I ENJOY THIS GIFT ALONE? I WANTED MY FELLOW-HUMANS TO HAVE A TASTE OF THE GOOD LIFE. (CHOMP-CHOMP.)
SO I MIXED SOME OF MY SERUM IN THE SPRING. WHEN THEY DRANK THAT WATER...
THEY TURNED TO ANIMALS. S HAVE YOU. THAT'S WHY YOU COULD INDERSTAND ALL THAT I JUST SAID.
(GASP!)
IT IS THIS CHEMICAL, ISN'T IT, THAT'S BEING MIXED INTO OUR SPRING? WHY DON'T YOU SHUT DOWN ITS FLOW THEN? AND DEVELOP AN ANTIDOTE INSTEAD?
I COULD. BUT IT WOULD MEAN THAT THE HUMANS WOULD TURN BACK. AND BE FORCED TO RETURN TO THE CARES AND TROUBLES OF THAT LIFE. I CAN'T BE THAT MEAN TO THEM.

OF COURSE YOU CAN'T. OINK! I BELIEVE I WILL JUST LIE HERE IN THE WATER AND LOLL ABOUT. YOU'RE RIGHT YOU KNOW... THIS IS THE LIFE. PEACEFUL AND WET.
MAYBE I CAN MAKE SOME BUBBLES TOO.
POOOOPPRRRR!
BLUB-BLUB-BLUB
UGHHH! EWW-YOU-YOU...
...YOU'RE POLLUTING MY SHRINE OF SCIENTIFIC SOLITUDE, YOU FART-HOG! GET OUT AT ONCE!
BAH-OINK... ZZZZ.
HE WON'T GET OUT! AND IF YOU DON'T START DEVELOPING THE ANTIDOTE, I WILL ASK HIM TO GIVE FREE REIN TO HIS DIGESTIVE TRACT. AND I'LL DO THE SAME!
SO WHAT? I WILL GO MAKE MY HOME ELSEWHE—
—YEOWWW!
WELL... DOES THIS CHANGE YOUR MIND? OR SHOULD I DRILL SOME BORES INTO YOU... BOAR STYLE?
POINK
FINE-FINE! YOU WIN! I'LL PUT IN THE ANTIDOTE. AND THEN I'LL JUST WALK OUT OF THIS MAD-WOOD, BACK TO THE HUMAN WORLD. AT LEAST THEY DON'T THREATEN TO TURN YOU INTO A BORE WELL!
THAT'S *BORE* LIKE IT! HAHAHA!
OINKZZZZZ!

SOON...
THIS IS GREAT, SHAMBU! THE ANTIDOTE WORKED! THE SPRING IS BACK TO BEING DRINKABLE AND MY PEOPLE HAVE BEEN RESTORED TO THEIR HUMAN FORM AS HAS MY SHANTI...
...LOOK! THERE SHE IS! JUST DONE WITH HER TRANSFORMATION.
HI, SHAMBU! HEEEHEEEHEEE!
HI!
OO-OO-AA-AA*!
HEEHEE. WE'VE CALLED THE FOREST RANGERS. THEY WILL BE HERE TO GET THIS FELLOW WHO WAS *MONKEYING* AROUND WITH OUR LIVES. HEEHEE.
UH... I THINK THE LAUGH IS A RESIDUE OF BEING A HYENA. IT WILL WEAR OFF IN A WHILE, WON'T IT, SHAMBU? HEEHEE?
UMM...
I DON'T KNOW. SHAMBU AND I DON'T SEEM TO HAVE ANY RESIDUES OF OUR ANIMAL FORMS, DO WE?
*ORANGUTAN-SPEAK FOR: "HOW DARE YOU DEPRIVE ME OF MY OWN ANTIDOTE? LET ME AT IT!"
ANYWAY, WE MUST ESCORT OUR BRAVE GUEST TO HIS WORLD NOW. LET'S GO.
UH... WHAT'S THE HURRY?
OH, BUT YOU MUST GO HOME. THE PORTAL CLOSES AT SUNSET. HEEHEE. COME.
OH, WELL... IF YOU INSIST. LEAD THE WAY...
...AND DON'T LOOK BOINK... ER... BACK.
END OF TAIL

SHIKARI SHAMBU: AN AXE TO GRIND

Writer Dushyant S.
Pencils & Inks Savio Mascarenhas
Colours Akshay Khadilkar
Letters Pranay Bendre

COME ON, OLD BOY. YOU CAN DO THIS. WE'LL START WITH A WALK, TAKE IT TO A JOG, AND RUN A LITTLE TOO!
SHAMBU SET OFF DOWN THE TRAIL—
NOW THIS IS A BEAUTIFUL DAY FOR A NEW START!
WELCOME TO THE WILD
BACK IN THE FOREST—
THAT'S RIGHT! CHOP 'EM DOWN, LADS!
CLOSE BY—
HUFF! YOU CAN DO IT, OLD CHAP! COME ON.
DROP

NO PAIN, NO GAI—**WHOA!**
SLIIP
THUD!
BONK!
AAAAAAAAH!
SPLASH!
HEEELLP!
UH-OH...

EEYAAA! THIS IS NOT THE RUNNING MOTIVATION I WAS LOOKING FOR!
PRRAAAAA
UP! UP! UP!
GOOD ELEPHANT, NICE ELEPHANT...
PHEW!
FLIP
THIS IS FAR DEEPER IN THE FOREST THAN I'VE BEEN IN A LONG TIME. HOW AM I GOING TO GET OUT WITHOUT A JEEP?

SUDDENLY—
SOME GOOD WORK TODAY, LADS. AT THIS RATE, WE'LL ALL BE RICH MEN!
WHO'S THAT?
AHOY! WHO ARE YOU PEOPLE? WHAT BRINGS YOU TO THE FOREST SO EARLY?
WHO'S THIS CLOWN?
ERR... WE'RE GOING ON AN EARLY MORNING WALK. YEP, WE'RE JUST SOME... WALKERS...

OH, FELLOW MORNING WALKERS! SPLENDID! SAY, COULD YOU HELP ME OUT? MAY I USE YOUR CELL PHONE? I LEFT MINE AT HOME.
YEAH, YEAH. SURE.

HELLO? RAJU AT BASE CAMP? I'M STRANDED IN SECTOR 9.
BASE CAMP? BOSS, HE'S A RANGER!
WHAT?! WHY IS HE DRESSED FOR THE OLYMPICS THEN? ANYWAY, **GET HIM!**

GOTCHA!
GULP!

PUT DOWN THE PHONE, RANGER!

BUT—
DIVE
HEY!

THUNK!

BOSS, HE'S MAKING FOR OUR SHED!
YAAA! NOT AGAIN!
IN THE DARKNESS, SHAMBU LED THE ANGRY BEAST TOWARDS THE LOGGERS' HIDEOUT.

AND—
BA-DAM
CRASH!
MY EQUIPMENT! NOOOOOO!!!

BY THEN, SHAMBU'S PHONE CALL HAD BROUGHT IN THE CAVALRY—
THAT'S MY BOYS! HUZZAH!
JUNGLE Rangers

ONCE AGAIN, SHAMBU, WE CAN'T THANK YOU ENOUGH. YOU SAVED THE FOREST FROM THESE FIENDS' AXES!
OH, IT'S ALL IN A DAY'S WORK.
SAFE TO SAY, SHAMBU DIDN'T GO RUNNING ON JANUARY 2!

SHIKARI SHAMBU IN ACTION!
Story & Script Sean D'mello
Pencils & Inks Savio Mascarenhas
Colours Umesh Sarode
Letters Pranay Bendre
I DON'T UNDERSTAND WHY I HAVE TO TAKE AN ACTOR ON A GUIDED TOUR OF THE FOREST.
HE'S NOT JUST AN ACTOR, HE'S ALSO THE PRODUCER OF A JUNGLE ADVENTURE!
THE MOVIE IS ABOUT A FOREST RANGER WHO TAKES ON POACHERS.
BAH! STORY OF MY LIFE.
THAT'S EXACTLY WHY THIS ACTOR/PRODUCER WANTS TO SPEND A DAY WITH YOU AND LEARN THE ROPES.
(SIGH) I HOPE HE'S ACCOMPANIED BY HIS HUGE ENTOURAGE; I COULD USE THE PAMPERING THESE ACTORS GET.
WELL, WE'RE HERE. GOOD LUCK, SHAMBU. MAKE ME PROUD.
SHAMBU, I'M RAHUL RAJAN. THANK YOU FOR AGREEING TO DO THIS.
HERO'S HUT
IT WAS UMM... MY PLEASURE.
SO CAN WE SET OUT FOR THE JUNGLE? I'M EAGER TO LEARN EVERYTHING I CAN FROM YOU.
SURE. WE'LL JUST WAIT FOR YOUR ENTOURAGE AND THEN WE CAN START MOVING!
YOU SEE, I'M NOT ONE TO ENJOY PEOPLE WAITING ON ME AND COOKING FOR ME, BUT I CAN UNDERSTAND YOUR NEEDS.
OH. THAT'S NICE TO HEAR BECAUSE I HAVE NO ENTOURAGE.
I WANTED TO CARRY MY OWN PACK AND LOOK AFTER MYSELF, LIKE A REAL RANGER. LIKE YOU, SHAMBU.
IN THAT CASE, LET'S START MOVING.
OH RATS!

THAT'S THE MOVIE ACTOR AND PRODUCER.
BOSS SAYS THEIR MOVIE LOCATION IS HAMPERING OUR SMUGGLING OPERATION. KIDNAPPING HIM WILL SCARE THEM AWAY. LET'S GO.
A FEW HOURS LATER...
YOU SEE, IN THE FOREST, YOU MUST ALWAYS BE AWARE OF YOUR SURROUNDINGS.
UMM, SHAMBU... BEHIINNNDDD YOU!
HISSS
YOU WAIT HERE; I'M GOING TO THE OTHER END TO CREATE A DISTRACTION.
I'LL GRAB THE ACTOR WHEN SHAMBU GOES TO EXAMINE YOUR DISTRACTION.
THIS TRUMPET SOUNDS EXACTLY LIKE AN ANGRY ELEPHANT TRUMPETING. IT SHOULD GET SHAMBU'S ATTENTION.
...PRRRRRRFFF!
AAAH! WILD ELEPHANT!
I THINK SCREAMING IS HIS TRICK TO DISTRACT THE ANIMAL. I MUST SCREAM TOO!
AAAH! WILD ELEPHANT!

OH MY, OH MY! I HOPE THAT ELEPHANT DOESN'T COME THIS WAY.
OH MY, OH MY. I HOPE THAT ELEPHANT DOESN'T COME THIS WAY.

I DON'T KNOW HOW THIS WILL SAVE US FROM THE ANIMAL, BUT WHO AM I TO QUESTION THE GREAT SHAMBU'S WAYS?

LOOKS LIKE THEY ARE DISTRACTED. I'LL GO NOW AND GRAB THAT ACTOR.

CRUNCH!
UH-OH!

THE ELEPHANT IS BEHIND US!
RUNNNNNNN!

AHHHHH!
OKAY, I GUESS WE'RE REALLY GETTING INTO RANGER MODE!

AHHHHHHHH!
WAIT, WHY ARE THEY RUNNING TOWARDS **ME**?
I HOPE THE ELEPHANT BACK THERE ISN'T CHASING US.

WHAT ARE THE TWO OF THEM DOING?
HE'S LOOKING BACK AND RUNNING. I DON'T THINK THAT'S SAFE!

THUD!
SHEESH! SHAMBU RAN STRAIGHT INTO A MAN.

OH! THIS MAN WAS MAKING THE ELEPHANT NOISES. PERHAPS, SHAMBU KNEW ALL ALONG!

WAIT A MINUTE! IF SHAMBU JUST CAUGHT THE GUY MAKING ELEPHANT NOISES, WHO STEPPED ON THE BRANCH BEHIND US?

THUD!

THAT WOULD BE ME. NOW, HOW WILL YOU EVER BE A GOOD RANGER IF YOU AREN'T ALERT?!

MINUTES LATER...
SHAMBU, WAKE UP.
FIVE MORE MINUTES, SHANTI. YOU CAN MAKE ME BREAKFAST TILL THEN!
SHANTI?

HUH? EH? RAHUL, WHERE ARE WE?
IN A PIT. TWO THUGS HAVE TRAPPED US, I'M NOT SURE WHY!

THERE THEY ARE! WHAT DO YOU GUYS WANT? MONEY? LET US GO. I'LL PAY YOU HANDSOMELY.
HA-HA! WE ARE NOT INTERESTED IN YOUR MONEY. WE'RE AFTER SOMETHING ELSE.

WE JUST WANT YOU TWO TO GET VERY COMFORTABLE.
VERY COMFORTABLE. BECAUSE YOU ARE NEVER LEAVING THIS PIT!

SHAMBU, THEY'VE GONE AWAY. WHAT'S OUR PLAN TO GET OUT OF HERE?
PLAN? I HAVE NO PLAN. I'M GOING TO GO TO SLEEP. THIS IS NICE!
HMM, SHAMBU HAS A PLAN IN MIND. I'D BETTER PLAY ALONG.
SURE, SHAMBU, LET'S GO TO SLEEP.
LATER THAT DAY—
WE NEED TO CHECK ON THEM, MAKE SURE THEY ARE WELL. THE BOSS IS COMING SOON.
UMMM, THEY DON'T LOOK TOO WELL TO ME.
THEY'RE HERE. BETTER STICK TO SHAMBU'S PLAN.
WHAT DO YOU THINK HAPPENED TO THEM?
THEY MAY HAVE PASSED OUT DUE TO DEHYDRATION. GO GET THEM WATER AND FOOD!
MINUTES LATER—
WE'LL LOWER THE FOOD BASKET TO THEM.
SHAMBU, THEY ARE SENDING FOOD DOWN. HOW DO WE PROCEED?
FOOD!
GIVE ME FOOD! I'M STARVING!
WHAT'S THE PLAN, SHAMBU?
PLAN? WHAT PLAN? I'M JUST REALLY HUNGRY!
AH, GOT IT!

HE'S PULLING US DOWN WITH THE BASKET!
LET GO OF THE BASKET, SHAMBU. IT'LL COME DOWN EVENTUALLY.

I DON'T HAVE TIME FOR EVENTUALLY. I WANT IT NOW!
SO THAT'S HIS PLAN.
GREAT IDEA, SHAMBU. LET ME HELP.

OH NO! NOW THE ACTOR IS PULLING THE BASKET TOO.
FINALLY, YOU ARE BEING USEFUL. PULL THE BASKET!
PULLING!

TUG
THERE IT IS. GOT IT.

AAAA

THUD!
GOOD JOB, SHAMBU!
I MAY NOT LOOK LIKE IT BUT... I ACTUALLY MOVE AS FAST AS A HARE.

COME ON, SHAMBU. LET'S GET OUT OF HERE BEFORE THEIR BOSS ARRIVES.
(SIGH!) I LIKE THIS PLACE. NO WORK, NO SHANTI BUT PLENTY OF FRESH FRUIT.

MINUTES LATER—
(HUFF-HUFF) FINALLY WE'RE OUT. WHAT A CLIMB.
HANDS UP! BOTH OF YOU.

THOSE TWO DOOFUSES CAN'T DO ANYTHING RIGHT. I'M MUKESH, THE RINGLEADER. NICE TO MEET YOU.
WOW. THE LIFE OF A RANGER IS SO ENTERTAINING.
ENTERTAINING?
WHERE ARE YOU TAKING US?
STOP TALKING AND START WALKING. I'M GOING TO GET RID OF BOTH OF YOU AND OF ALL MY TROUBLE.

WE'RE GOING FOR A NICE NATURE WALK WHICH WILL END WITH BOTH OF YOU WALKING RIGHT OFF A CLIFF.
SHAMBU, ANY PLANS TO HELP US GET OUT OF THIS ONE?

ULP! NO. I JUST CAN'T BELIEVE MY LAST MEAL EVER WAS A BOWL OF FRUITS.

OKAY, WE'RE HERE. NOW JUMP OFF OR I'LL SHOOT AND GRAVITY WILL DO THE REST.

ANTS! ARMY ANTS. THESE GUYS BITE!

ARMY ANTS? WHAT ARE YOU TALKING ABOUT?
THESE ANTS CAN DO MORE DAMAGE TO US THAN A FALL EVER COULD—AHHHH! GET THEM AWAY!

GREAT GOING, SHAMBU! THAT WAS SOME QUICK THINKING!
THUD!
WOAAHHH!

HAVE THOSE ANTS GONE?
YES, AND SO HAS MUKESH. WELL DONE, SHAMBU!

IT'S A SHAME THAT I'LL NEVER BE ABLE TO USE ANYTHING I LEARNED TODAY IN THE MOVIE.
YOU WON'T? WHY NOT?

EVEN AN ACTION DOUBLE WOULD BE TOO SCARED TO TRY ANYTHING YOU DID TODAY!
OH, I SEE.

SHAMBU, ONE LAST THING. DO THOSE ANTS BITE BADLY?
THE ARMY ANTS ARE THE SCARIEST OF ALL ANTS. ONE BITE CAN CAUSE AN IMMENSE AMOUNT OF PAIN.

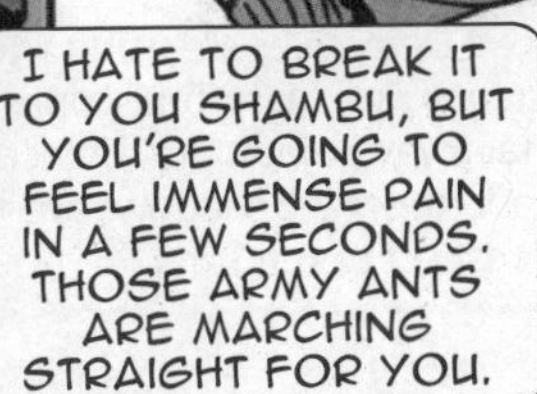

I HATE TO BREAK IT TO YOU SHAMBU, BUT YOU'RE GOING TO FEEL IMMENSE PAIN IN A FEW SECONDS. THOSE ARMY ANTS ARE MARCHING STRAIGHT FOR YOU.
AHHH!

READERS SAY

Shikari Shambu is the best beast-fearing, animal-loving pseudo hunter ever!
– Kaavyashri Rao, Mangaluru

I really want to know where Shambu gets his luck from.
–Atharva Date, Pune

I could really use some of Shambu's luck. ☺
–Karthik Vinayan, Kerala

Shambu is a legend, a hero and a foodie. I wish I was more like him. I'd love to take a walk in the jungle with Shambu and learn about animals!
–Temsumenla Pongen, Nagaland

Shikari Shambu is my favourite character because he's so brazy (brave + lazy)!
–Elia Kulsum, West Bengal

Shikari Shambu has made me fall in love with animals... but, of course, from a safe distance!
–Swarnil Bhattacharya, Tripura

ANSWERS TO PUZZLES

Reunited (Pg. 14)

Cupcake Catastrophe (Pg. 52)

Shambu is holding a fork in his hand with a bowl of soup. Soup is eaten with a spoon and not a fork. This is why Shanti suspects Shambu of eating the cupcakes!

Wrongful Scenery (Pg. 37)

(1) The Defective Detectives are using a telescope instead of a magnifying glass. Telescopes are only used to view far away objects, not objects close by.
(2) Shambu's and the tree's shadows are in the wrong position with respect to the Sun.
(3) Tantri cannot have a lit match underwater.
(4) Suppandi cannot mow the grass with a vacuum cleaner, that too when it is unplugged.